To my dear
friend
Keep
Judy

Relative Stranger

By

J. R. Cahn

This book is a work of fiction. Places, events, and situations in this story are purely fictional. Any resemblance to actual persons, living or dead, is coincidental.

ISBN: 1-4107-9728-7 (e-book)
ISBN: 1-4107-9727-9 (Paperback)

Library of Congress Control Number: 2003096591

This book is printed on acid free paper.

Printed in the United States of America
Bloomington, IN

1stBooks – rev. 10/24/03

Acknowledgements

A special thank you to my dear friends who provided honest criticism and encouragement. Without you, I could not have completed this book.

For those who are my life and make me who I am,

To Chaya for her sensitivity and editing style

To Efraim for his brutally honest insights

And to Jeff—my partner—for his unconditional support

In memory of Shlomo Zalman & Yosef Pinchas

"Then Jacob kissed Rachel; and he raised his voice and wept. Jacob told Rachel that he was her father's relative..."

Genesis 29: 11-12

"Do what you feel in your heart to be right, for you'll be criticized anyway. You'll be damned if you do and damned if you don't."

Eleanor Roosevelt

1

Rachel was having trouble shifting in her seat, her feet tightly confined by the overstuffed backpack on the floor. Everyone in the cabin was asleep, but Rachel was too uncomfortable and her thoughts too disturbing. It was impossible for her to think of how she could survive for fourteen hours across the Pacific. At barely five feet tall, she considered it almost humorous to even think that she could feel so cramped in a seat.

At any other time in her life, she would have been excited about traveling halfway around the world to Australia. Having accepted an invitation to speak at a conference, she had the opportunity to get away from home - alone. How could she not experience a thrill as she viewed the monitor that tracked the flight across the equator and the dateline? The Xanax didn't help her relax and her stomach still ached.

Rachel remembered leaving Kennedy Airport with the terrible knot in her stomach. The memory of her previous day's visit to the nursing home would not fade. It remained in her mind, so vivid that she was afraid to close her eyes. He was so thin and could barely speak. He did not recognize anyone - not her husband, not her mother, and not her. The voice that emanated from his emaciated body was one she had never heard before and would never hear again. He yelled at the physician with all his strength. Panic—or was it a confused anger that resounded. "I don't understand!" he yelled. "I don't understand!" No one could understand and perhaps no one ever would.

Constant worry ran through her veins. The man Rachel had left in the nursing home was so different from the man she had known, with whom she could talk about anything. Throughout her life, he was always interested in her and she had known for years that he bragged about her accomplishments. And he was the only one who would really listen to her, even when she was an obstinate teenager so long ago.

No one ever asked Rachel's uncle why he never married. No one ever asked him why he chose to live with her grandparents until they died. No one ever asked to visit his apartment. Everyone knew not to ask. Everyone respected his privacy and his wishes. No one wanted to pry. They all said "That's Jake."

And how he loved Rachel's children! After Rachel's father died, Uncle Jake stepped into the role of grandfather. Filled with pride at every school performance. Laughing with joy while reading their report cards. Thrilled to attend Rachel's son's little league games—and watch as his grandnephew caught the final out to win the championship. She remembered how he talked about that game for two years, describing every detail of Adam's facial expressions, describing how the bases were loaded, describing how all the kids ran to him, easily lifting him onto their shoulders. The entire team triumphantly parading Adam around the ball field after the ball—somehow—miraculously—had landed in his glove.

Rachel would later come to realize, though, that he never spoke about himself. Her uncle was a fantastic listener. And the reality was that she really didn't know her father's brother as well as she thought.

2

As she fumbled with her keys holding grocery bags, Rachel tried to contain her two screeching school-age children who were stooped under the weight of their own backpacks. It was close to five and Rachel had to unpack the groceries and start dinner. The bags were strewn around the kitchen floor while Rachel reached into the fridge to rearrange items on the shelf. The most inopportune moment for a phone call.

"Rachel, it's Mom." The urgency in her voice compelled her to stop what she was doing to listen.

"I'm at the doctor's office with Jake, downtown. He asked me to drive him down this afternoon because he didn't feel well. He complained of a headache and has been hiccupping non-stop." Rachel almost giggled at the thought of hiccups. "I waited while the doctor examined him and then the doctor called me in. Jake was outstretched on the table, bare-chested, in an unusually deep sleep, mouth open, snoring loudly." She continued, her voice quivering with panic. "They haven't been able to wake him up. I suggested an ice pack and tried slapping his cheeks. The doctor, Dr…Dr…oh, his name will come to me…anyway; he doesn't seem to know what to do and wants me to take him home in this condition. I can't handle it." Her voice changed to defiance. "And I'm not going until he is awake enough to walk to the car. The nurse finally let me make this long distance call to you because you are listed as next of kin."

The groceries cluttering the kitchen became a blur. "Okay. Calm down." Rachel replied. "Listen, if you're going to take him back home with you, call me when you get there. I'll drive down to get him. I know doctors here who can help. He'll probably need a gastroenterologist, at least to figure out the cause of the nonstop hiccups."

"Fine." Her voice was still shaky. Rachel could not control her fear. "I'll call you then. Bye."

Rachel hung up. She didn't quite understand what was unfolding, but she knew her mother could not accept responsibility to care for a brother-in-law. Not that she would want to anyway. There was no one else to call. By default, Rachel inherited the responsibility, though she barely understood the severity of that obligation.

David walked through the door to the garage around 6:30. He dropped his briefcase, draped the cleaning over the staircase banister and headed across the kitchen to the bathroom. "Uncle Jake is sick," Rachel blurted. "Mom is driving him home from the doctor's office when he becomes conscious. He's been out cold for two hours already. They could not wake him up. I'm just waiting for the call so I can go get him."

"You're going tonight?" he responded as he washed his hands. "Alone?"

"Yeah. I'll be fine," Rachel answered, not believing a word of what she said. "What else can I do? Mom can't take care of him. She has her own difficulties getting around. Just stay here with the kids." The kids were in the den watching TV and were more quiet than usual. They must have sensed something was wrong.

David looked tired from a day at work and hadn't expected to be left alone with the kids. As he began to unknot his tie Rachel couldn't help but notice how distinguished he'd become. David stood tall compared to Rachel's height, although his 5'10" physique was average. His chest had broadened since they had met 15 years ago, the result of his daily swimming regimen. His receding hairline had turned into moderate baldness and there was some gray at the temples. Their years of marriage had been tested a lot, with all sorts of family stresses. Yet, through it all, David's commitment to family was always a given. Rachel knew he would be there to help, yet she felt guilty about the added strain on their already hectic lives.

David sat in a kitchen chair, his right leg crossing his left. "I'll try getting in touch with Norm," referring to a gastroenterologist. "Maybe he can see Jake tomorrow."

The kitchen phone rang but once. "It's Mom. We're home. I have Jake sitting at the dining room table and I'm trying to get him to eat something. I'm talking to him constantly so he stays awake." If it weren't such a serious situation, Rachel would have felt sorry for Uncle Jake having to listen to her mother's ramblings.

Rachel grabbed her purse and keys and turned to her husband as she passed him on her way out the door. David made her stop for a hug, the type of hug that always made her feel safe and protected. The momentary pause for assurance gave her the additional strength that both he and Rachel knew she needed. The concern on his face was obvious. Exaggerated by fatigue, Rachel's voice was barely audible. "Thanks. I'll call you from Mom's." She stood on her toes to kiss him.

3

It was a chilly April night and it seemed especially dark on the roads driving from Connecticut through Westchester. There was an occasional drizzle and the rhythmic, intermittent click of the windshield wipers put Rachel in a daze. Although she was concentrating on the road, she could not remember how she got as far down as the Cross Westchester Parkway. She was worried and frightened of what was ahead. Already mentally fatigued from the demands of family life and work, she did not want to face more demands of her time. She was tired. She was always tired. All she wanted to do was escape. Run away to some foreign land. Her trip to Australia was already planned, but it wasn't until July…

The car exited the parkway and seemed to execute the turns automatically toward the Hutch. As Rachel made the last right onto North Street, she found a parking space pretty close to the building. She ran up the block and up the driveway of the building hearing the faint honk behind her, confirming she locked the mini-van with the remote.

It took only thirty-five minutes. She must have been speeding.

Mom looked weary when she opened the door. Fatigue weighed heavy on her face. With tremendous relief in her voice she greeted Rachel. "Am I glad to see you!" She motioned her head toward the dining room. As she closed the front door, Rachel noticed that her mom's limp was more pronounced. That hip must be hurting a lot.

An older man of average build was sitting at the dining room table with his head slumped forward. Jake would probably be better described as being on the shorter side of average. His colored brown hair was messed. His shirttails were hanging out and the stubble on his face was visibly gray. Rachel realized immediately that her uncle certainly did not look like his normal self. Always modest in his dress, often wearing older, worn clothes, he was always neat and well kept. In fact, he had always looked significantly younger than his seventy-five years, perhaps because he never married and had no children. Those responsibilities didn't exist in his life. Then again, Rachel didn't know much about his private life, so her assumptions were just that—assumptions. But for the first time in Rachel's life, she saw her uncle looking his years.

His body jerked every time he hiccupped. At first Rachel was surprised. The child in her almost laughed. But the hiccups didn't stop and the spasms looked painful. She realized this was serious.

"Hi, Uncle Jake." Rachel was conscious of the sound of her voice. He grunted his simple reply, "Hi, Rachel."

"Mom called and told me that you're not feeling well. Let me take you back home with me and we'll get you to a specialist tomorrow morning. How long have you had these hiccups?"

"Since Saturday." His voice was a barely audible monotone.

This was Monday night! He'd been feeling poorly for a few days now. Jake was not one to say he didn't feel well or bother to go to a doctor. He *really* must be ill. He didn't want to talk and Rachel didn't want to bother him, so she left him at the table and walked into the kitchen. Mom seized the moment to relate all the details of her day. She was pretty agitated but Rachel knew she needed to calm her mom first before calling David to find out what the gastroenterologist had suggested.

Mom droned on. "…Finally, Dr. Elner—that's his name—I don't know why I couldn't remember it when I called you."

"Never mind, Mom. Go ahead."

"Okay. Finally, Dr. Elner came out and asked me to come with him because he 'wanted to show me something.' Then he took me into his office and pointed to Jake stretched out on the table. Well I told you about that on the phone. But he was in such a deep sleep and snoring so loudly…"

"Yeah, you told me about that."

"Alright. Just listen," Mom raised her voice. She was impatient, too. "The doctor thought we should just let him sleep it off. He told me that he had taken a cardiogram and that his vital signs were normal. He had given him a shot of Demerol, actually half a dose, and then he asked me who Rachel was. I told him you're my daughter, Jake's next of kin."

It took all of Rachel's patience to hear her tell the story again. Every detail weighed heavily on Rachel's ears. She looked through the kitchen door into the dining room. Jake mumbled that he wanted to sit on the sofa. She watched him as he got out of the chair, very shaky on his feet. Rachel's impulse was to run and help him, but Jake always was so independent and private that she had to control herself; she didn't want to insult him in any way. He staggered and fell back onto the sofa.

"Jake, do you feel strong enough to walk downstairs and get in my car?" Rachel asked, anxious to start driving home as soon as possible.

"Give me a few minutes," he answered. She strained to hear the words he spoke.

"Rachel, give him some more time," Mom interjected. Let's wait another half hour. Come into the kitchen. Do you want something to drink? Soda? Coffee?"

"I'll take some soda." Rachel walked over to the fridge and took out a can of Diet Coke.

"Here's a glass." Mom swiftly took a glass from the cabinet as Rachel flipped the tab on the top of the can.

"Don't bother, Mom. Tell me the rest of the story at the doctor's." Rachel was trying so hard to hide her own fatigue and impatience. She glanced at the clock. 8:30. She hadn't eaten dinner and her stomach was rumbling. Mom continued. "...The doctor, nurse and receptionist hadn't tried anything. They didn't know what to do. They thought he probably could sleep the remainder of the evening, but of course, immediately added that he couldn't remain at the office. I told them in no uncertain terms that I would not take him until he was coherent. Finally, they got him to sit in a chair but watched so he wouldn't fall forward. He finally seemed to come around."

Rachel sipped the soda while her mom kept talking. She needed to talk. This experience made her extremely nervous and upset and Rachel assumed her mom would rely on Valium to help. She is too dependent on that drug, Rachel thought, but that is a separate issue. Rachel stood observing the reality of her mother's and uncle's advancing ages and it pained her.

"Meanwhile, I asked them if I can call you and the receptionist hesitated when she heard *Connecticut*, a long-distance call. I had to remind them that you're listed as next of kin, so she finally dialed. After I spoke to you the doctor asked if I had help at home. There was no question in my mind that Jake could not go back to his apartment, yet the doctor didn't feel this was a hospital case!" Mom got angrier as she continued. "I told the doctor I had a doorman and the doctor actually suggested that if I had trouble getting him upstairs I should call the police. He repeated that twice! I got Jake in my car and the doctor supposedly helped by buckling his seat belt. Then the doctor came up to me to thank *me* for my help. Soon after, I noticed that Jake was not strapped in properly and I had to stop in traffic, get out and adjust it myself. Finally I drove home. The doorman kept an eye on him while I parked my car. Jake walked like he was in a stupor; drunk, not speaking clearly, not thinking clearly."

Rachel couldn't listen anymore. "Did the doctor give you any instructions?"

"Yes. Here. What he should and shouldn't eat. He said to be sure to get Jake to a gastroenterologist soon because Jake had complained of some obstruction while eating. I just assumed that Jake hadn't eaten. Even though he said he had no appetite, I insisted he eat two soft boiled eggs and sip some tea."

Rachel tuned out whatever else her mother said as she examined the papers from the doctor. Besides the Demerol the doctor gave him at the office, he had written a prescription for Valium. "All this would really knock him out," she thought. She called home.

"Hi, David. It's me." Rachel described the state Jake was in and briefly summarized Mom's experience. "Did you call Norm?"

"Yes, he's not home. I spoke to his wife and she's getting in touch with him. She expects him home soon."

"What do you think I should do?"

"I'll try to reach him again while you're driving home," David said. "Meanwhile, don't give him any other medicine," he added.

Rachel had to get out of there. "It's time I get going, Mom. We still have a ride back to Connecticut. Let's see if he can get downstairs. Then I'll pull the car around." Rachel took charge.

She then walked into the living room and emphatically called out "Jake!" so he would respond. He lifted his head, slowly, confused. "Let me help you on with your coat and let's go downstairs."

He looked like he was getting up in slow motion, as he braced himself with his hands on the sofa on either side of his lap. He still was very unsteady. It was obvious that he had not been able to wash and care for himself. His trench coat needed to be cleaned and, as Rachel helped him on with it, she noticed the lining was frayed. The three took the elevator downstairs and the doorman helped Mom with Uncle Jake while Rachel brought the van around. Jake stepped up into the van, sat behind the driver's seat and Rachel buckled the seat belt around his waist.

"G'bye, Mom. I'll be in touch. Thanks for your help."

Rachel spent the return trip to Connecticut praying that Uncle Jake wouldn't slump over in the seat or that anything else more drastic might happen. After all the time spent criticizing her mother, Rachel ended up doing the same thing in a desperate attempt to keep Uncle Jake awake. She just kept talking. She wouldn't shut her mouth. Talking about the route she was driving. Talking about the kids. Talking about anything. When they were a few blocks from home, Rachel called David from the car to make sure he would be ready to come out and help Jake from the van and into the house. David got Jake undressed and helped him into bed.

4

Rachel was jarred from a very deep, exhausted sleep. Was it a dream or was someone calling her name? She glanced at the clock, perplexed. 6:50 a.m. She knew David would not be calling her. He is usually over at the synagogue for morning services. And it wasn't a child's voice. As she became more alert, she focused on the sound of the voice. Remembering the events of the previous night, Rachel recognized the voice of her uncle. The demanding tone straining to yell her name frightened her.

"Rachel!! Rachel!!" She heard it over and over.

Rachel jumped out of bed, threw on her robe, and flew down the stairs as the back of her robe flapped behind her. She looked at the bed in the den. He wasn't there. He called out again. She needed to locate the source of his screams. Rachel opened the door to the bathroom and a wave of dread enveloped her. The lump in her throat almost hurt as she tried to hold back tears. She knew she had to appear in total control. *Why wasn't David home yet?*

Uncle Jake was lying on his back in the tub with his legs dangling over the side. He had fallen backwards as he attempted to stand by the toilet to urinate. Wearing just a pair of boxer shorts, his body appeared thin and frail. His appearance triggered Rachel's memory of how her grandmother looked when she was Jake's age. Rachel was not thinking clearly. She just moved quickly toward him.

"I can't turn to get up," Jake said, frightened. His eyes were filled with terror and embarrassment. The tub was too slippery for him. He was looking around frantically for something to grab onto to brace himself. Without a moment's hesitation, Rachel bent down and put her arms around his body. With all her strength, she lifted him up and out of the tub, totally ignoring the sharp pain radiating down her back and leg.

"What happened?" Rachel's voice quivered, but only she realized it. She helped him walk back into the den and he got back into bed.

"I'm not sure," he said. "I don't remember." I remember getting up and walking to the bathroom. But I must have fainted. Maybe because I haven't eaten for three days." Jake look tired and depressed, but mostly he was embarrassed. From what Rachel did know of her uncle, he didn't want to be dependent on anyone and now he was obliged to be dependent on her. He never wanted to *bother* anyone or permit anyone to enter his private life. He probably didn't tell the doctor that he hadn't eaten for three days, either.

David returned from synagogue. He walked through the front door with his head down reading the front page of the newspaper he had picked up from the front walkway. He was startled as Rachel approached, no doubt surprised that she was awake at such an early hour. He looked up with a puzzled expression. Rachel told him how she found Uncle Jake in the tub.

The doctor insisted that Jake get to the Emergency Room as soon as possible; the ER would be notified that Jake was on his way.

And the ER is where Rachel spent the rest of the day. Reluctantly, she became an intruder into Jake's personal life as she filled out the paperwork, and removed Jake's Medicare and Insurance Cards from his wallet. Even writing his birth date made her feel awkward.

As Jake went for tests, Rachel waited and paced. She felt she could not leave him alone. She was his only family.

Unaware of how much time passed, she heard a familiar voice from the nursing station asking about Jake. "What are you doing here?" Rachel walked over to greet David. He was holding a brown paper bag. "I thought you could use a break and I brought you some lunch," he replied. Rachel gave him a big hug. She was sure he saw her tears. It was at that moment she realized that she had not taken off her coat since she arrived at the hospital at 8:30 in the morning.

Rachel's body relaxed as David put his arm around her shoulder and led her toward the cafeteria. Walking through the hospital hallway, Rachel caught a glimpse of her reflection in a glass door. Her short, brown hair was uncombed, limp and in need of a shaping. The top was falling flat and it didn't have the bounce it usually had when properly cut. She was overly self-conscious about the twenty pounds she knew she had to lose and frequently wore a loose overshirt with her jeans. The reflection was brutally honest. She looked chunkier than she thought.

They were approaching the cafeteria. "I don't know anything yet. Were *you* able to find out anything?" Rachel asked. "Not yet," David answered.

David bought her a diet soda, took some coffee for himself and led her to a table not too far from the registers. The bagel and cream cheese tasted good. Rachel was hungry. "There's not much you can do by sticking around here," David said. "Why don't you go home and the doctors will call you when they know something."

"No. I'd prefer to wait until he's at least admitted to a hospital room. Let me stay with him until he gets settled. The kids have a key. They'll let themselves in after school. Just call them and let them know I'll be late."

They spoke of other things while they ate. David tried to distract Rachel from the realities of the hospital. "I was pretty busy with patients during the morning, but we managed to finish on time for lunch. There was this one lab case that came in late, though, and the guy needed his bridge before leaving on a business trip. Susan had them express it over and it ended up working out okay." Rachel listened with half an ear as she watched others on their lunch break—doctors, nurses, hospital personnel, visitors. She ate rather quickly and David walked her back to the Emergency Room. Jake had been taken for x-rays.

At three in the afternoon, Jake was admitted to a room on the third floor. Rachel left for home soon after.

5

"Mom! Telephone! Line one!" Abigail shouted in a singsong from the other room. "It's the doctor!"

"Hi Rachel. It's Steve Katzen."

"Yes. Find out anything?"

"Nothing definitive since I admitted him this morning. I'm having a kidney specialist look in on your uncle. His sodium levels are very low. Life-threatening low. It could be the cause of the hiccups. I'm also having a pulmonologist examine him because the x-rays indicate something by the lung. He'll be in the hospital for a few days—at least. We'll need to run more tests to determine the cause of the low sodium. We're not sure of anything yet."

Rachel sighed. "Thanks for calling me, Steve. Just keep me posted. You can call me at home or at work. I'm usually in the computer lab during the day. Thanks, again." Rachel did not understand what was unfolding and she did not want to talk anymore.

A little while later, David came home from the office. “Did you hear from the doctor?” David asked as he dropped his briefcase by the chair, forgetting how annoyed Rachel gets when she has to move it to set the table. “Yeah, I did. But my mother’s biting comments upset me more. She called just before the doctor.” Rachel threw some silverware on the table.

“Uh oh.” David looked almost pained having to ask the next question. “What now?”

“I’ll summarize. She told me that I don’t have to stay with Uncle Jake all the time. She actually said ‘You didn’t run and sit with Dad that often.’”

Zing. Just what Rachel didn’t need…a dig through the heart.

“Did you answer her?” David asked.

“After biting my lip so hard I thought it would bleed, I responded more civilly than she deserved. I told her that we don’t have to go through that again and to let me handle what is happening now.” Rachel continued, agitated. “It’s incredible, David. Mom continues to resent me for not being able to travel to New York more frequently during Dad’s last months. She’ll never let me forget it.” Her voice drifted. “It’s absurd,” she whispered shaking her head in disbelief.

6

The man at the desk was animated and speaking with his hands. She was standing behind the counter and seemed totally oblivious to the stacks of books behind her and the piles of books on either side of her that took up most of the counter space. There was a small clear area of counter directly in front of her. She smiled at the man who was talking. Her eyes looked directly and honestly at him as she maintained that sweet smile on her face. As she listened, she nodded, causing her brown, shoulder length, wavy hair to fall forward ever so slightly, gently touching her perfectly arched-shaped brow.

A smile, he thought. It seemed like forever since he had seen anyone smile. The war was over, but the tension was still in the air. It was all so confusing to him, but he was drawn back to Eastern Europe, compelled to get any information he could about family. He felt deeply obligated to learn whatever he could for his parent's sake.

His memory of his journey from Europe to New York was but some vague and distant images from the perspective of a four-year-old child. In 1929, his mother received permission and whatever documents were necessary for her to travel with her two sons to reunite with her husband in New York. The family had been separated from him for nearly two years until he was able to bring them over. Now, just shy of twenty years later, even though his parents and brother advised against his travel back to the Europe they escaped, he was here, waiting in a crowded office to begin his search for family members; searching for any information about who did or did not survive the heinous crimes against humanity about which the world had just recently learned.

There must be at least twenty-five people ahead of him, he thought. But he didn't mind waiting. He was tired from his cross-Atlantic journey and he was fascinated watching the people around him. He was compelled to travel here, he thought, in much the same way as they were. All of them were here for the same reason. Survivors, looking for information about loved ones. Mostly, though, he spent his time observing her. Her manner was patient and her reaction understanding. She was multi-lingual, and he presumed, highly educated. As each individual approached and told their story, she seemed to know which book or documents to refer to and provided a response that, for the most part, appeared to satisfy the individual inquiring. Even if it was but a tidbit, a clue, so there was continued hope for additional information.

He could only see the upper part of her body. She was wearing a perfectly ironed white, button-down, man-tailored shirt with the collar resting comfortably over a gray cardigan sweater. Although her ears were pierced, she wore no jewelry. He tried not to stare, but he was stricken by her smile and the brightness of her eyes. She wouldn't be considered beautiful, he thought, as Hollywood might have defined beauty. But she had a simple, genuine radiance about her, a kindness, and she displayed compassion to each person she helped. Her movements were graceful as she turned pages of large books and selected other books from the shelves behind her. Everything she needed was within her reach. Occasionally she would disappear for a few moments only to reappear with another large book in her hands. She seemed just as comfortable as he always felt surrounded by books.

The number of people in the waiting area diminished and he was one of three left. The hours had passed quickly as his mind wandered. Finally, he was standing at the counter just about three feet from her, looking directly at her as she smiled at him. His mind wandered to his journey from Europe as a child. The family smiled when they reunited in New York, but there were no smiles after his uncle died. His mother's baby brother died of pneumonia. The family was never the same again. There were no more smiles. They lived through the Depression. They lived and feared World War II. Fatigue overwhelmed him and the present uncertainty of learning the realities about his extended family caused a wave of anxiety that swept through his entire body. His knees buckled and the room began spinning. He blacked out.

7

Rachel had known Elizabeth for thirty years, almost as long as Jake had known her. Rachel remembers meeting her for the first time when she was a young teenager. A soft-spoken, petite, woman with short straight gray hair simply cut, Elizabeth joined the family at Passover Seders every year. She accompanied Jake to every family event including Rachel and David's wedding and more recently, Abigail's Bat Mitzvah. Rachel came to learn that Elizabeth didn't have any family in the United States, having come from England as a young woman. Her British accent always sounded so pleasant to Rachel's ears. But Rachel got quite an earful from that soft-spoken woman when she called early one morning the same week Jake was admitted to the hospital.

"Rachel!" Elizabeth sounded forceful. Perhaps it was just the fear in her voice. "What's going on with Jake?"

"Hi, Elizabeth." Rachel recognized her voice immediately. "He's in the hospital. Didn't my mother call you?"

"Actually, I called her. But she was rather abrupt with me, practically rude."

"Well, these past few days, she's been through a lot, too." Rachel couldn't figure out why she was making excuses for her mother. She certainly had more important matters to worry about.

"What happened?" she asked. Although Rachel always considered herself an impatient person, she found herself having enormous patience with Elizabeth and reiterated the previous day's events. Yet Elizabeth questioned her over and over. "What causes this?"

"I don't know. He's going through lots of tests. Let's see what we find out. I promise I'll call to let you know."

"You know I saw him on Saturday."

Rachel knew that Jake saw Elizabeth every Saturday, no matter what; sometimes on Sunday, too. This was one of the few facts she did know about his personal life. They always went out on Saturday. That had been their schedule for years.

Elizabeth sounded guilty, upset. "He didn't feel well, then. I told him he should see a doctor. But you know Jake. I can't force him to do anything."

"I know, Elizabeth," Rachel replied, with a tone that indicated she understood exactly what she meant.

"I've noticed changes in him for a long time now. He has been more argumentative. I thought he should talk to a doctor and he just quipped 'You're not normal, either.' So I just kept quiet. I was considering distancing myself from him, you know, for my own sake. For my own survival." There was shame in her voice.

She hesitated and meekly questioned, "Rachel, have you ever been in his apartment?"

"No."

"Really?"

"No one in the family has ever been in his apartment since he moved in fifteen years ago. I can only imagine what condition it's in."

Elizabeth jumped in, "I've offered to help him clean it. I've even suggested that he should have someone come in to clean for him. He'd always laugh."

"I've offered to help him with his apartment, too. I know he never unpacked the cartons from my grandparents' house. That's why he could never give me my grandmother's candlesticks, one of the few precious items she brought with her from Europe."

"Will you please let me know when you hear something about Jake? I'm very worried."

"Yes. I promise."

Rachel felt badly for her. Elizabeth had sounded terribly worried. Jake and Elizabeth were close friends, companions of sort, although no one knew much about their true relationship. Emotions were running high and Rachel had no intention of becoming a go-between for Mom and Elizabeth.

8

The dinner dishes were left in the sink and that was good enough for Rachel to leave the kitchen. She was anxious to be alone in her office to call her mother.

"So you spoke with Elizabeth?" Rachel started the phone conversation. "She seemed to think you were abrupt, asking personal questions."

Mom chuckled. "Of course she would say that. She divulged things to me about her relationship with Jake that she regrets saying. She actually told me that he didn't *satisfy her*. I questioned her only because I was curious if it was his problem or hers. She said it was her problem, because of her anatomy or something, and that was why he couldn't satisfy her." She paused. "That must've done wonders for Jake's ego." The biting sarcasm in her voice was thick.

Rachel heard more than she wanted to hear, but Mom went on. "Elizabeth told me she had noticed changes in Jake for months now and wanted him to go to a doctor. She even told me she was trying to distance herself from him. Why wouldn't she *help* him instead of distancing herself? What kind of friend is that?" She was raising her voice. "When I asked her why she didn't let anyone in the family know, all she could say was 'You know Jake. He would've *killed* me!'" Mom took a breath. A little less agitated now she added, "I don't know, Rachel, but if it's a matter of health, what could she be afraid of? So he'd yell. So what?"

"Look. I didn't hear the conversation that went on between the two of you, but I spoke with her and I told her I would let her know what the doctors find. The only thing I found a bit irritating was that she kept asking me the same questions over and over and I'm not a doctor. I don't have any answers."

"Call her only when it's convenient for you, Rachel," Mom insisted. "Don't put yourself out for anyone. You have enough on your plate for now."

Boy, she was right about that.

Rachel hoped her cheerfulness would not appear as phony as it felt, but walking through the hospital halls triggered all sorts of anxieties. She kept her eyes focused upward on the colorful Mylar Get Well balloons David carried as they walked into Jake's hospital room.

"Hi! How are you doing?" Rachel forced herself to sound cheerful.

"Hey! Where have you been?" Uncle Jake asked.

"We're here now, Uncle Jake," David quickly retorted.

"Yes. I see." He was distracted for the moment. "And the balloons!" He chuckled. "Well, well…"

"I see the hiccups subsided," Rachel commented.

"You know," he said speaking very slowly and deliberately, "I noticed I hiccup when I eat anything or just take a sip of tea."

"But you need to eat something, Uncle Jake," Rachel blurted without thinking.

He didn't answer. Rachel walked around to the other side of the bed, near the bed table, and noticed that Jake's right forearm and elbow were covered in an awful shade of purple with yellow. It was black and blue from his fall in the tub.

"Does your arm hurt?" she asked.

"No, it's just bruised." He moved his arm and hid it under the bed sheet. Uncle Jake looked thin and frail in the hospital gown, reclining in the bed. Tubes were connected to various parts of his body. The IV was his sole source of sodium and sustenance. He hadn't eaten for days.

Again he asked, "Where have you been?"

"I was with you all day yesterday in Emergency and right here this afternoon. The kidney specialist was here to see you—a Dr. Frank. He tried to get you to stand up, but you fell back on the bed…you…well…I guess you could say that you fainted."

"I did?" he exclaimed. "Gee, I don't remember that."

"They attribute your memory loss to the low sodium levels. You'll be going for some tests tomorrow to examine the lungs." He looked up, surprised. "What do the doctors say?"

"Honestly, they haven't said anything. They're waiting for test results."

"I wish they'd come and talk to *me*." He was frustrated and angry. Obviously he wasn't used to being out of control and confined to a bed.

The dinner tray was delivered.

It was quiet. Rachel looked over at David but was unable to read his face. David quickly changed the subject to the news and offered to go downstairs to the gift shop to get a newspaper for Uncle Jake. Rachel was left alone by Jake's bedside.

She dutifully unwrapped the foil from the plate and moved the hospital bed tray over to Jake. He sat up.

"Want some of the mashed potatoes?" she asked.

Jake took the tiniest taste. As he swallowed, the hiccups returned. Frustration was written on his face. He threw the plastic spork back on the tray and pushed it away. "These…these…What do you call it?" He asked through the spasms.

"Hiccups," Rachel replied softly, very unhappy that he was so frustrated and uncomfortable.

"Yes…yes…that's right…hiccups." He closed his eyes for a while.

"Did you find my reading glasses?" Jake asked a while later, again through the hiccups. It was difficult for him to complete a sentence without a few spasms. "They might be by the bed at your house unless you find them in my coat or jacket pocket."

"I haven't seen them but I'll check," she assured him.

"They were a magnification of about 2.75, but I wanted to try something stronger. If you can't find those glasses, maybe you can buy me a pair. I'll repay you."

"Don't be ridiculous. Just let me know what you need and I'll pick them up."

"I think they go up to 3.25. Try that. When can you bring them?"

"Sometime tomorrow."

Rachel had always known her uncle to have his face in a newspaper, magazine, flier, or book. He was an avid reader, often spending an entire day sitting in the library. She always assumed that was how he spent most of his days—just reading. Whenever he came to visit when she was a child, he would come into the apartment and walk over to the piano bench that was piled with the newspapers from the previous days. He would lift a section and read it standing up. That was the stance that remains embedded in her memory: Uncle Jake holding open a newspaper, head down.

He never watched television, shocking in today's society.

David returned with the newspaper, but Jake didn't seem too interested. Maybe it was because he couldn't read the newsprint that well or the hiccups tired him.

The dialogue shifted and Rachel casually mentioned that Mom was picking up his mail. It was then Jake sat up in bed and began to shout defiantly. Rachel couldn't remember ever hearing him so angry.

"I knew something like this would happen! Why does she have to do that? Why does she have to be so nosy? Always controlling everything! Yeah, and then she'll want to pay the bills!"

Rachel and David exchanged puzzled facial expressions. What a strange reaction, Rachel thought.

He was always close with Mom. And why would *anyone* want to pay someone else's bills??

"I know she was trying to help and I thought it would be okay," Rachel said, trying hard to placate him. "If you don't want her to open anything, that's fine. I'll tell her to just throw the envelopes in a bag. You can't leave your mailbox overstuffed."

"I don't understand." He strained to sit up; the hiccups were making it difficult for him to complete a sentence. "I've had Bobby hold my mail for up to two weeks!" He leaned back against his pillow again. "See what arrangements you can make."

Rachel knew very well that she was not going to drive to his building just to talk to the doorman about the mail. As long as Mom was willing to help, she will let her drive the five minutes from her place to get his mail.

Jake sat back, visibly unhappy, and shaking his head. David read Rachel's face and knew she was hurt. Uncle Jake never yelled at her. David knew Rachel was taking this too personally and she was not ready to face the fact that her uncle was truly ill.

David tried to ease the tension. "Do you need anything else, Uncle Jake? We can order the TV for you."

"No. No TV service. I'm tired. Thanks for coming. Thanks for all your help."

Rachel took her purse and turned to Jake. "I'll see you tomorrow. Get some rest."

The casino-like sound effects emanating from the twenty computers running educational games in the school computer lab the following morning was almost deafening. Rachel didn't hear the phone. A teacher called her from across the room. "Rachel!—phone!" She could barely hear the man's voice at the other end of the line. It was the pulmonologist. Test results indicated that some blood was found in Jake's pleural cavity.

9

"I'm terribly embarrassed. Very sorry." His voice was soft and he could barely bring his eyes to meet hers.

"There's nothing to be sorry about," she answered softly. Her English was excellent. Her European accent was captivating. "People journey long and hard to get information about loved ones. It is a difficult time and extraordinarily emotional. Please do not apologize. Can I get you some more tea?"

"Yes, thank you." He hadn't realized how long it had been since he had anything to eat or drink. Certainly, that contributed to his weak feeling. His body was probably still recuperating from that awful pneumonia-like illness he experienced during his stint in the army. Although his hospitalization at the army base in the States worried his family, at least that illness prevented him from being shipped overseas to

the front lines. He couldn't even think about how fearful and worried his parents would've been.

She returned with the tea and some pastries. "I'm basically finished for the day. How can I help you now?"

"You've already helped me. You've given me as much information as possible, I presume. Unfortunately, there just isn't much to go on until all the towns and names can be collected in one place. The towns and cities I had known as a boy were totally devastated by the war. It's not even two years since the war ended. Who knows what documents and listings exist. I don't want to go home empty-handed, though. I have to learn something about my grandparents and aunts and uncles."

"Perhaps I can get some more information tomorrow. I have to admit and I am sorry to say that it looks pretty grim. I can call a few of our other offices and see if they have any additional lists or records from the DP camps. And there has been a concentrated effort to rebuild as quickly as possible. People yearn for a return to some sense of normalcy and sanity. In the meantime, where are you staying?"

"I don't know if I can extend my stay for another day while you continue to try to gather information about my relatives." His voice was soft but determined. "But may I show you my gratitude for your help? Is there any decent place around here where I could take you to dinner? That is, if you don't have any other plans."

"Thank you for your kind offer. I'd like to..." she hesitated.

He quickly interrupted her, "I'm sorry. I'm not usually so bold. I'm very appreciative for your kindness and I'm never this forward. But I feel very comfortable talking with you and since I do not know anyone here..."

She was flattered. There was something about this man. He was decent looking, well mannered and charming. He did not look like a survivor of the Holocaust trying to return to his home. He had traveled from America to locate family! No one travels to a Europe that has been left torn and tattered. If they're lucky, people leave Europe to travel to America.

No, there was something different here. A haunting sadness in this man's grayish blue eyes that she couldn't quite define. She was intrigued.

"Let me go home and check on my father. I just want to make sure he has dinner and then I can meet you at the American Restaurant. It's about two blocks west of the inn. Is 8:15 good?"

"8:15 is fine."

10

Rachel spent her days visiting the hospital or on the telephone. Calls from doctors. Calls from family. Calls from friends. Jake's friends. Mostly female friends. Rachel had vague recollections of some of their names mentioned over the years; others were totally unfamiliar. A few names she recognized as members of the book club he had been involved in for years. And, of course, Rachel spoke to Elizabeth who called frequently wanting every detail of what every doctor said, constantly questioning, wanting to know the causes of the symptoms. Rachel's patience waned.

Uncle Jake didn't have many visitors, only Rachel and David, occasionally with their children, Abby and Adam, and Rachel's mom.

The hiccups continued. The spasms made it difficult for Jake to talk. When he did, it took him a long time to get words out. The diaphragm spasms were visible—hard, violent hiccups that forced his upper body to convulse. When he was medicated, the hiccups subsided, and he slept heavily.

When Rachel saw him awake, he would ask her to contact one or two of his friends. He was very specific making sure she understood whom *not* to call because this one or that one will ask too many questions and pry for too much information. "You can stay on the phone with *her* for over two hours! Don't waste your time," he warned as he laughed about it.

At home the telephone rang constantly but Rachel had no answers to friends' inquiries. He's going through tests: CAT Scans, EEGs, MRIs, X-rays, EKGs, blood tests, and biopsies. This went on for over two weeks. Uncle Jake continued to hiccup; he stopped eating. Both Rachel and David silently understood what the doctors were looking for but it was never discussed.

Finally, as Jake's sodium level reached a normal range, so did his clarity of thought. His hiccups stopped. A limited appetite returned. And the doctors never found the source of blood in the pleural cavity. One of the pulmonologists actually had the nerve to tell Rachel that the reason for the lung problem may be just "intellectual curiosity; that we may never know what caused it."

That type of medical insight did not comfort Rachel. She was frustrated and angry. That doctor certainly lacked any of Patch Adams' compassion. There had to be *something* causing all these bizarre symptoms…

The doctor discharged Jake from the hospital to a nursing home so he could recuperate and regain his strength. His sense of humor returned along with his eccentricities. He packed his few belongings from the hospital including all the unused straws—about twenty-five of them—from his food trays and four oranges in their original plastic serving bowls.

Jake seemed far less agitated once he had Rachel's long distance calling card number. He kept himself busy with calls outside the local area. Rachel never questioned him about whom he called or where he was calling. She was brought up knowing to respect his privacy and she felt that this was the least she could do to repay the generosity he had always shown toward her family.

He was more than satisfied with the pair of reading glasses Rachel bought. She had selected the most conservative style—brown frames, the half glasses that fit lower on the nose. Actually, it made him look like quite the intellectual and very professorial. He laughed when Rachel teased him about it.

Rachel accompanied Jake as he waited for the ambulette that was to transfer him to the nursing home. They were left waiting at the hospital all afternoon until Rachel learned that the ambulette was stuck in traffic. Uncle Jake looked terribly depressed as he sat at the edge of the bed fully dressed anxious to leave and Rachel couldn't bear to watch his discomfort. The nursing home was just across the parking lot, yet hospital policy required an ambulette to take him there. Rachel had made quite a fuss at the nurses' station, for naught.

Decidedly, Rachel walked from the nurses' station to Jake's room and motioned for him to walk with her. Grabbing a blanket from the bed and wrapping it around his shoulders, the two walked off the ward together and into the elevator as if they were two kids sneaking out of school. Casually, Rachel looked over her shoulder as she walked down the hall with her uncle. No nurses or other hospital personnel were in sight. She drove over to the nursing home and within five minutes Rachel and Jake shared a good laugh as he settled into his private room on the third floor. He made Rachel feel like a heroine.

The room in the nursing home had pleasant appointments furnished with a cherry wood dresser, bedside table, TV and closet. Rachel had bought him some new clothes, unpacked them and neatly placed them in the drawers. As she unpacked, Uncle Jake examined the few pairs of pants, shirts, pajamas, socks, and slippers with a sense of excitement like a little boy receiving a big bag of toys he wanted all at once. The new pants were left out so Jake could try them on. He laughed as Rachel knelt to pin the hems. Who knew when he felt pampered last? She took the pants to the tailor the very next morning and brought them back to him properly tailored by evening.

David and Rachel continued to visit Jake frequently. He was feeling better and now wanted to regain control of his life. He needed some items from his apartment, most importantly his checkbook.

And now the inevitable time had come. Jake had to ask Rachel and David to go to his apartment. No one—absolutely no one—had ever been in his apartment. This was the ultimate compliment from Jake, Rachel interpreting her uncle's request as a sign of his complete trust. He was thankful and he knew he had no choice but to become dependent on them. But Rachel was very uneasy about what they would find.

The family thought they had some idea of the condition of his apartment. They knew there were boxes left unpacked from when he moved out of his parents' apartment, as well as some others belonging to his aunt from when he was executor of her estate.

He did try to warn them. He warned that they wouldn't be able to open the door very much. "Maybe David could fit through it. You have to move your body sideways to get into the apartment," he said. Shifting his eyes toward Rachel, he said, "But you might have trouble." Rachel didn't respond and neither did David although he made a mental note to ease his wife's anguish about her self-image later.

Jake continued. "My checkbook is in the kitchen on the left side of the table under envelopes. The key to the car is right by the door. As you are facing the door to leave, put your hand under the pile on the floor on the right and you'll find it."

They left the nursing home planning to go to Jake's apartment the very next day. David didn't miss a beat. "Honey, don't let what Jake said upset you. He's been sick. Let's just focus on getting him what he needs."

Rachel didn't say a word and entered the elevator.

None of the warnings prepared them. Using the set of unfamiliar keys that had hung on a hook in her kitchen cabinet for years, Rachel unlocked the door. David pushed against it. He pushed far enough for them to fit their bodies through the door sideways. He turned on the light and Rachel shrieked, her body trembled. She could barely let out the scream from her throat that was reverberating in her head. She was hysterical. She couldn't breathe and tears streamed down her face, uncontrollably.

They never expected such a sight.

David courageously climbed on top of the piles of papers and bags—all garbage—slipping passed cartons, in an attempt to get further into the apartment. Not even a thread of carpet was visible, only a sea of bags upon piles of dirty old papers, envelopes and boxes. Envelopes, once white, appeared gray and black with filthy dust, inches thick, resting atop everything. David somehow maneuvered his way into the kitchen, coughing every so often. He flicked the switch. The kitchen was the same—filled to capacity with papers, every piece of mail, fliers, newspapers accumulated over fifteen years. All in addition to the cartons of things he never unpacked. The kitchen table was piled three feet high with envelopes. Paper bags within plastic bags were filled with more envelopes and papers. Throughout, spaces that weren't covered with papers and envelopes were covered with more cartons still tied with the original cord. The boxes lined every inch of wall space. Rachel and David couldn't see any furniture. Papers and garbage were filling every inch of the one bedroom apartment.

Rachel was unable to move from the doorway, paralyzed by the shock. Deep down she knew there was something terribly, terribly wrong.

David climbed over the bags and cartons to get to the refrigerator. He found lots of cottage cheese and yogurt containers. As he opened them, *he* finally reacted, exclaiming, "Oh no!"

"Rachel! All the containers are filled with garbage. He didn't throw out food garbage, either!"

Rachel couldn't cope, wanting to run away from this nightmare that became her responsibility. She was nauseous. David persisted. He grabbed a bag and emptied the refrigerator. Working as a team, Rachel stretched over to take the garbage from David's outstretched arm and she ran with it down the hall to the incinerator chute.

When she returned, she mustered the courage to join David and together they climbed and slid across the piles of garbage strewn throughout the apartment. They peeked into the bedroom only to see more of the same. The bed was piled with stuff. Clothing was thrown on top of bags. There wasn't any way a human could possibly get to a closet, much less open the door. Only half the bed was void of clutter; just enough room was left for Uncle Jake to lie down. Rachel didn't understand any of this. She couldn't understand how anyone so wonderful could be living in these conditions and it frightened her.

"He can't come home to this!" Rachel blurted out, hysterically. David shushed her, intent on getting what Jake needed and getting out of that apartment.

On the way out, David found the checkbook and the keys exactly where Jake had described. They were surprised to find them. It was a warped sense of relief for them to know that their uncle did remember exactly where he'd left those items.

David whisked Rachel out of the building, passed the doorman's station and out onto the street. They drove to a nearby restaurant so Rachel could regain her composure. She was still visibly shaken. Trying to hold back her sobs, she excused herself from the table and went to the ladies' room in an attempt to clean herself up, rid her body of the thick, filthy dust and musty odor still in her nostrils, fearful that the dust was now in her lungs. She kept coughing. Maybe *that's* what got him sick, she thought.

Their return trip to Connecticut was quiet. Only the sounds of the radio could be heard, but every station played the same music. Every so often David glanced over to look at his wife and whisper, "I'm sorry, Rach. I'm so sorry." Holding the wheel with his left hand, he massaged the back of her neck with his right as she wept.

By the time they reached home, they were both more composed. The long drive helped. The children demanded their attention as soon as they walked in. They always had a way to distract Rachel and to keep her busy. David had bought take-out; dinner was ready within fifteen minutes. The kids finished eating in no time at all and scattered to other parts of the house to their own evening activities—homework, TV, Nintendo, and IM's.

The phone rang soon after dinner. Rachel picked it up in the kitchen, completely surprised to hear Uncle Jake's voice.

"How was Mount Olympus?" Jake started.

"I've come down from the mountain!" Rachel responded with a phony Southern twang, trying to impersonate a preacher. As Uncle Jake was trying to hide his shame, so too would she hide her true feelings to help Jake maintain some dignity.

"We got everything you asked for. We'll bring it over in a little while. How are you feeling?"

"Okay. But I really want those things."

"Let me just get the kids settled and I'll see you soon."

"Oh…oh sure. Take your time, then…And thanks."

As Rachel hung up, David knew by the look on her face that she was barely holding it together.

"Don't say anything, David. We *have to* go deliver his things tonight. And no, I can't wait until tomorrow."

"Take it easy, Rachel. I'm not arguing with you."

11

He kept his eyes on her throughout the dinner. He hadn't smiled and laughed in such a long time. It didn't seem right to enjoy himself in a country that had been so severely damaged physically and emotionally and left scarred by war. But she was with him at dinner and he was enjoying her conversation. She, too, was hanging on his every word.

By his manner and eloquence, she realized he was highly educated and assumed he had studied at universities in America. His parents must be very proud of him, she thought. They started a new life in a new country, and their son was able to attend good schools. Not many got that opportunity so quickly. His dry wit amused her. He wasn't pushy or loud. He loved books, newspapers, magazines, anything he could get his hands on to read. He focused on minutia; little details that she would not even consider. He had a completely different angle and perception about the mundane.

She felt comfortable with him. And safe. Yet she hardly knew this gentleman seated across from her in the restaurant. But she felt she did. And she learned to trust her instincts years ago. In much the same way she trusted her instincts by not accepting the offer to work at the university. She was much better off at the UNNRA. After all, look how the university ended up treating her father after so many years of devoted teaching. Forcing him to retire because he verbalized his opinion—a different opinion from that of the administration. Her father was never the same since he left his post.

"Dessert?" he asked. "Would you like to share a piece of the Bavarian Cream Pie?"

"Sure," she answered, with a big smile that lit up her entire face. She looked like a little girl waiting for a piece of candy.

"And two cafes," he added, holding up two fingers.

She laughed. He was trying to make himself understood.

"My father..." she said softly. "My father became a different man because of the war. He detests inhumanity and voiced his opinions within the university. Not only was he forced to leave his post, but also invitations for article submissions and guest lectures stopped completely. It has been difficult for him to rebuild his life. He is no youngster and his eyes have dulled. Ach, but enough about me. I should be grateful I have him with me still..." Her voice tapered off.

12

Uncle Jake was already dressed when Rachel picked him up from the nursing home at 6:45 in the morning. He was anxious to be on time, clutching a blue velvet *tallis* bag with his prayer shawl carefully folded inside. She drove the car around the circular driveway to the entrance. He got in. "Does it usually start on time—at seven?"

"As far as I know."

As a woman, Rachel was neither obligated nor was she particularly interested in getting up early to get to the synagogue.

"You know, I once heard a wonderful explanation as to why a *minyan* is made up of ten men and does not include women," Rachel began.

"Yeah?" She had his attention.

"A rabbi once explained that a *minyan* is actually a quorum of ten *individuals* who share a common obligation. Since men are obligated to perform commandments that involve time, only men are included in that quorum. Women are not obligated for any commandment involving time because, like me, they are busy pushing the kids out the door in the morning so they won't miss the school bus!" Uncle Jake laughed.

Rachel made a left turn into the synagogue parking lot and drove up to the entrance.

"I'll be right here at seven-thirty," she assured her uncle.

"Okay, thanks." As Uncle Jake walked deliberately toward the entrance and opened the large glass door, Rachel took a deep breath and drove away. Today was her grandfather's *yahrzeit*—the anniversary of his death, and Uncle Jake insisted on getting a temporary release from the nursing home so he could go to *shul* to say *Kaddish,* the mourner's prayer, for his father. Uncle Jake was one to take family obligations seriously. He had been very devoted to his parents and very devoted to his brother, helping to care for Rachel's dad until the day he died.

Jake had gone to synagogue every day for eleven months to say *Kaddish* for his parents. Five years ago, he said *Kaddish* for his brother. Jake was especially devastated after Rachel's dad's death. He had lost his big brother and the last member of his immediate family.

Rachel returned to the synagogue exactly at seven-thirty. She watched as men of all ages exited the building. Some nodded hello to her, others came over to the car to chat. She waited. Five minutes. Ten minutes. Fifteen minutes. She parked the car and entered the synagogue. Uncle Jake was taking his time meticulously refolding his prayer shawl and placing it in his bag. Patiently, Rachel waited until he walked toward her and together they walked to the car.

"They gave me an honor this morning, calling me up to the *Torah* during the service. I thought that was nice. As I stood at the *bimah*, one or two of the men seemed to know me. One man even asked me if I had been in the hospital! Did he know that from David?"

Her eyes were on the road as they drove back to the nursing home. "I suppose David might have said something because prayers were said for you while you were in the hospital." Stopped at a red light, Rachel looked over toward Uncle Jake's face and then to his hands. "Uncle Jake, you're still wearing the hospital ID tag bracelets on your wrists. That's how they knew you were in the hospital."

Jake looked at his wrist, chuckling softly. "Yeah, yeah."

13

Rachel's family continued to visit Uncle Jake daily. Her children brought him cards and drawings. They knew he felt better when he told them he had found the library on the first floor. Although they would have thought it unlikely, he also requested a VCR to watch some movies—some oldies—especially Westerns. Perhaps he had enjoyed the originals in the theater many years ago.

Often they would find him sitting fully dressed at the table, reading glasses down on his nose, taking care of paperwork. Rachel continued to bring him his mail, unopened. Working on his paperwork, he looked more like a doctor than a patient.

But Rachel reiterated to the doctors, to the social workers, to the nurses, to anyone who would listen, begging them not to allow him to return to his apartment, describing the conditions, the details that haunted her daily.

"Rachel," the doctor eventually addressed her concerns with a firm but sympathetic tone. "I understand how you feel, but legally you cannot tell anyone how to live. I don't have any medical reason to keep him in this facility. He can be discharged in a few days. We can try to arrange to have a Visiting Nurse service look in on him at home and then they can deal with it through the Adult Protective Services. I'll speak with the social worker."

No one seemed to listen to her. But what hurt most was that she couldn't share her worries openly with her uncle, the very man who needed the help.

Rachel had delayed long enough. She found herself stammering, surprised she was so nervous talking to a man who she could talk to about anything, about work, family, difficulties with the kids, even difficulties with her mom. It didn't take long for her to figure out that she could tell him anything about *herself.* They never spoke about *him*, where he went, how he spent his days. She didn't want to anger him by bringing up sensitive topics. Or have him think she was prying. He was still recuperating. But she was the only family he had now and she knew he had to rely on her.

"Uncle Jake," she started slowly, hesitating, practically whispering. "I have some serious things to discuss with you. I don't feel terribly comfortable bringing this up, but I think it's important."

Slowly, he lifted his face from his reading and removed his reading glasses.

"Yes, what is it?"

Rachel noticed how put together Uncle Jake looked, much like his old self. His hair was combed and he was wearing one of the new button-down shirts with a new pair of pants.

"Well…I really feel awkward speaking to you about these things. But a few things are on my mind."

"Okay. Go ahead. Share them with me."

"Okay." Rachel took a deep breath. "The first is the apartment. Can't David and I help you or can we hire someone to help you organize things and…?"

"Rachel," he interrupted. His voice was serious, but not angry. Rachel was surprised—and relieved. She knew this was such a sensitive subject, but she also knew that he understood that she had his best interest at heart. "Yes, I've thought about it. But I'm feeling better now and I'll be able to do it myself—a little at a time."

David opened the door and entered the room. "Did you start your discussion?"

"Yes, I told him we were willing to help him at his apartment."

Jake addressed them both. "I've done it before. Really. I'll spend a little time each day and in about three weeks it will be much better. I'll even let you come down to visit then."

Not wanting to anger him, Rachel tried to add a cute tone to her voice. "You mean I can visit you at your apartment the first week of June and you'll have it done? You'll let me in?"

Jake laughed quietly, "Yes." It was heart wrenching. Rachel knew there was no way anyone strong and healthy, even thirty years his junior, could clean that apartment in three weeks. Certainly, they could not imagine him bending and lifting. "What are the other things you wanted to talk about?" he asked.

"Well…" Rachel looked down and picked at her nail cuticle. "You ought to consider having your paperwork in order—like a Power of Attorney and a Will. Do you have a Will?" Rachel lifted her eyes and looked directly at Jake. He was looking down, depressed. His body language made it clear that he didn't have anything in order. "You know, David and I have a Will."

He looked surprised. "You do?"

"Sure. We have kids and we wanted to be realistic and make sure all contingencies were covered. It is not pleasant and I was not very happy about dealing with it, but it is something we had to do."

Jake nodded. It was difficult to determine whether any of the conversation was penetrating. After a very long, uncomfortable pause, he responded. "Here's some paper. Why don't you write down the name of your friend—your attorney—and I'll think about it."

Rachel scribbled her attorney's name and phone number on his pad and dropped the subject. It was uncomfortably quiet for a while. Jake looked up, a pained expression on his face.

"What's the matter?" Rachel asked.

Jake's chin was on his chest. "I guess I'm not fifty anymore," was his barely audible response. Mortality was too difficult for him to face.

"Uncle Jake, you haven't been fifty for twenty-five years…"

He nodded. It wasn't until months later, looking back on that moment, that Rachel would realize just how much emotional distress Jake was experiencing. He had postponed important matters for so long and lacked the ability to face realities of life and at that moment he was embarrassed at being found out.

"Anything else?" he asked Rachel.

"Nope. Not right now."

Uncle Jake continued, "Well I want to talk to *you* about something now." His voice was deep and serious.

That took Rachel and David by surprise. They had no idea what was on his mind and they had spent their time worrying about how they could broach their concerns.

"Did you speak with Miss Conte?" Jake asked Rachel.

"Yes. She called me. She's the social worker who is working on discharging you Friday."

"Yes, well, she came to see me today. She arranged to have a Visiting Nurse come on Monday. She didn't even talk to me before she made the arrangements! I won't be ready to have her come into my apartment on Monday!"

Rachel realized that the doctor had heard her concerns about Uncle Jake's apartment. But she totally neglected to consider the effect this would have on Jake.

"What's to get ready?" Rachel said, trying to sound as naïve as possible, even though she felt the guilt rising to her throat. "She'll just check to see how you're doing." Rachel knew very well that he didn't want anyone walking into his apartment. No surprise. Jake didn't answer her question. He continued his thoughts.

"I've already arranged a follow-up visit at Dr. Tatarsky's office in ten days. What do I need a nurse for?" He paused. "Then I thought to ask your Mom if I can meet the nurse at her apartment so she can examine me there. It would just be for a few hours. I have her key. I'd stay there until the nurse left, then I'd go home."

Jake would plan anything to avoid the apartment issue. Rachel had already heard about this from her mom who didn't feel comfortable with Jake's idea for a few reasons, and Rachel couldn't fault her. The intent was to get someone from some agency to see the way he lived so he would be forced to deal with it properly. Rachel knew she tried to get that to happen, too. But more importantly, her mom didn't want to get involved so as not to become the responsible party for him. She did not want any social services agency to assume she could care for him legally or financially. She had made that decision for herself.

Jake got Rachel's attention when he raised his voice. "Your mother said, 'No!'" Now he was shouting. "I've always helped her when she needed me to open the door for the housekeeper before she returned from vacations or wherever. Or to drive her to or from the airport, acting as her personal chauffeur. I know why she said no! They call it 'tough love.' She's being ridiculous!"

He was angry and frustrated. He was angry at his life, and mostly, embarrassed about his apartment. He never had to answer to anyone before. He wanted support so he could continue to do things his way. Because of his failing health, he was losing control over his own life and he was going to fight to get it back.

"If you're really unhappy about the Visiting Nurse service, why don't you call them from home and postpone it? You can say you're staying with *me* for a week and you won't even be there." No sooner had Rachel said it did she regret it. She had been the one who had spent hours on the phone arguing with social workers and doctors, pleading that they not send him back to his apartment. They were the ones who agreed to handle it through a Visiting Nurse service. But Jake looked tremendously relieved. Rachel had given him an out, and his facial expression and mood changed completely. Rachel slumped in the chair, stunned at what she had done.

Even though the tension broke, Rachel had created her own stress by negating everything she had tried to do. Soon, Jake and David were back to normal conversation and Rachel joined in describing her travel plans to Australia.

"Is David going with you?" he asked.

"No, someone has to stay in the States to be available for the kids, even though they will be away at summer programs. Remember, David just had back surgery in March. It'll be too difficult for him to travel such a long distance."

"What if you can arrange coverage for the kids? I'll pay for David's trip. How much is it—five thousand dollars?"

"Oh no. The airline ticket was much less."

The offer was tempting. But David knew his wife needed to go on this trip alone. They had gone through a difficult year, living from family crisis to family crisis, and Rachel needed time away by herself. David really wanted to join her, but both of them knew that a parent had to be around for the children. They had mixed emotions about their uncle's offer.

David and Rachel exited the two large glass doors of the nursing home that automatically opened and headed toward the parking lot. "He's always been so generous with us," Rachel said softly.

"You do know that he's never let me repay him for helping us with our house," David said. "I've made out so many checks to him and he insisted that I void each one."

14

"So was your father all right?"

They had gone for a brief after-dinner walk that lasted over an hour.

"Yes, he was just fine. Since my mother died a few years ago and he lost his university post, he has aged quite a bit. I'm an only child and I worry about him a lot. We're very close and I usually have dinner with him after work."

"Don't you ever go out with friends?"

She chuckled and looked down. Although she was in her mid-twenties and had her degree from the university, her petite frame made her look even younger than her twenty-four years.

"My friends think I'm too serious, too intense. I get a lot of satisfaction from my work although it is emotionally draining these days and I'm usually engrossed in my reading. When I have time off during the day, I'd prefer to read or to wander alone in a

museum, rather than waste my time flitting around with giggly friends." She added, "They say they are friends, but after my father lost his position, they stopped coming around much. My father has noticed but hasn't said anything, although he does drop an occasional hint suggesting I go out more with people my own age."

He was so unsure of himself. He had never felt comfortable with a woman nor seriously considered taking her in his arms. But then again, he had never felt anything that even resembled passion before. He just met this woman, but he became intoxicated by her and he was finding it difficult to exert enough control to wait until he would see her again...if he could ever spend more time with her. His funds were already running low since he had to stay extra days to continue his search for family survivors.

"Come upstairs with me." He couldn't believe the words came out of his mouth. He was holding her and, as he breathed, he made sure to inhale a little slower and longer so her aroma lingered throughout his body.

She blinked her almond shaped eyes and whispered a barely audible, "Yes."

15

"Look at this. I can get this for twenty cents less in the other place," Uncle Jake complained.

"Perhaps. But did you ever stop to think about how much you're paying for gas driving from one store to the next for the cheaper prices?" Rachel answered. "This is convenient. It's right next-door. You have to take care of yourself. You've just come back from the hospital!"

"I suppose you're right. But…"

Rachel had stopped at the supermarket to pick up a few things for Uncle Jake to have in his apartment. He had been very surprised that David and Rachel emptied his fridge when they were there to pick up the items he requested. He was still in the nursing home when they had to explain that they didn't want any food to spoil or have his house smell when he returned. He didn't disagree, although the conversation had turned a bit bizarre. They merely caught a glimpse of a paranoia he was experiencing, but they were not astute enough to define it as that at the time.

"You threw out everything?" he asked, incredulous.

"Yes. We didn't want anything to smell."

"But where did you put the empty jar of gefilte fish?"

"In the recycling box."

"But they'll know it's mine!"

"How?"

"How many Jewish people are on the floor?"

"So? No one cares about your garbage!"

Rachel and Jake continued up and down the supermarket aisles. "What else do you need, Uncle Jake? We have a few bananas, the cereal, and yogurt. Do you need tuna or sardines? Oh yeah. You told me they were on sale before you got sick and you stocked up."

Her rambling continued. "I don't mean to be a nudge and I don't want to disturb you in any way, but will you please call me just to let me know how you're feeling. I don't want to keep calling you and risk being a bother. Maybe you'll be asleep."

Uncle Jake smiled, understanding that his niece cared. "I'll have the answering machine pick up so I can hear who is calling. Sometimes there's someone who calls who I know will keep me on the phone for over an hour. But, yeah…, yeah…I'll call you," he assured her.

It was terribly difficult for Rachel to believe that she would soon be dropping Uncle Jake at his apartment building, leaving him to return to that apartment. She couldn't do anything more for him and she had to let him go with his dignity intact.

The calls came in daily, as Uncle Jake promised. Although he didn't talk much about anything, it seemed as if he wanted to keep Rachel on the phone. Just to talk. Just to be in contact with a non-judgmental voice. Rachel always tried hard not to offer him an opinion about how he should do things. That is, unless he specifically asked. Jake appreciated that.

The discussion usually started out with a description of what he ate during the day. He complained that he was still weak but he will start his "clean-up project, a little each day." He found himself sleeping late, having some yogurt in the morning, and then going out to the deli for a late lunch. He would have soup and then bring a half a sandwich back to the apartment. Rachel remembered when David threw out a lot of *half sandwiches* from Jake's fridge.

He called daily for about a week. Then, when he began to complain about not being able to eat, Rachel convinced him to call the doctor.

"I'm driving up on Monday for my appointment with Dr. Tatarsky."

"Well, how about staying over and then driving back in the morning? I don't think you should drive both ways the same day. Give yourself a rest. You're welcome here."

"I'll think about it. Maybe."

Uncle Jake did drive to his appointment on Monday. But he did not clearly understand or recall the doctor's instructions about what he was allowed to eat. Uncle Jake refused to eat anything. Tea was about the only thing he would try. He agreed to stay over.

At 7:40 a.m., Abby and Adam got on the school bus and Rachel left for work, very proud of the children for not having awakened Uncle Jake. They had quietly eaten breakfast and left the house. Uncle Jake was still asleep when Rachel drove off.

The morning passed uneventfully until Rachel heard that David was trying to reach her. The school secretary was trying to locate Rachel and called all over the school. All Rachel heard was "urgent."

"David left a few minutes ago to find your uncle," David's receptionist said. "Your uncle called and said he was calling from the *mall*, that he didn't feel well—to come get him. He said he's near mailboxes and flags. Apparently, he fainted and someone near the phone picked it up to talk when Jake became conscious. Jake took the phone back and told David to come and pick him up. So now David is at the mall."

Rachel's heart raced. "How can I get in touch with Jake or David?" The computer lab was a large enough room for Rachel to pace. She was filled with worry and didn't know what to do except wait. Rachel overlooked the fact that someone had canceled her next class.

Finally, after what seemed like an eternity but was only twenty minutes, the phone rang.

"David!"

"Listen. I'm at the mall. I've looked all over. I've been to every entrance. I've been to the side on State Street near the flags. I've looked up and down the streets. I've worked with security and police looking all over the mall. I've even driven throughout the garage—all seven levels. Rach, I can't find him."

"I don't know what to do! Should I meet you and help you look?" Rachel's voice cracked.

"No. No. I'm going to go back to the office and wait to hear. That's all we can do."

"I have to do something. I'm going home. Maybe he'll get back there or he'll call."

"Okay. I'll talk to you later. I'm going back to the office."

Rachel grabbed her bag and ran out to her car. When she got home, the phone was ringing.

"Rachel. Listen." David's voice sounded urgent. "I just heard from Uncle Jake. He's at the Rainbow Center. When he said mall, I just assumed the *Mall*. Anyway, he's by the mailboxes and phones. There aren't any flags there. I don't know what he thought he saw. I hope he's okay. He waited to call my office again—get this—because he didn't want to bother me if I had patients!"

"That sounds like him. Okay. I'm on my way."

In two minutes Rachel found Uncle Jake sitting in his car, head forward, his chin on his chest. She pulled her car in the space just to the left of his. He looked up when she called his name.

"Rachel! I've been waiting…"

"We couldn't find you! When you said *mall* we thought you meant the big Mall near the highway. I assumed you stopped off for something before going home." Jake shook his head as she spoke.

"What!? Why would I do that? I came here to go to the drug store to buy a case of that drink—you know—with the nutrients. That's all. I got up late and got a late start." He started to open the car door but stopped. "Let me follow you home."

"No way." Rachel was emphatic. "Why don't you get into my car and I'll drive you back to my house. David and I can pick up your car later."

Uncle Jake didn't have the strength to argue and allowed Rachel to help him into the car. He was able to walk into the house without assistance and sat, slumped, at the kitchen table. She placed a cup of tea before him. A short time later, he headed toward the guest room and slept for most of the afternoon. The doctor had scheduled a CAT scan for him the following day.

Rachel sat up in bed, startled as she heard David running downstairs. The clock illuminated 5:50 a.m. Only muffled voices could be heard from the room below. It was difficult to awaken…

David opened the bedroom door. "We have a problem. Uncle Jake fainted again. I heard him calling my name. It just happened while I was in the bathroom getting dressed."

"Where did he faint?" *Like that made any difference.*

"In the hall between the guest room and bathroom."

Now she was fully awake. She threw on a robe and went downstairs with David.

"You can't drive him over to his appointments today, Rach. You'd almost have to carry him! You can't drop him off and leave. What if he faints in the building just getting to the doctor's office? No. We have to call for an ambulance now. He's very weak."

Rachel went into Jake very quietly. He was lying on his side, his arm raised behind his head to support it. The side of his head was resting on his forearm. The black and blue marks on his forearm from his first fainting incident had healed. She spoke slowly, clearly and deliberately. "Uncle Jake, we have to get you back to the hospital. We have to find out what's happening. We're calling an ambulance now."

"I have a test scheduled for today," was his only concern.

"I've already canceled it. They'll take care of it in the hospital."

All his strength was sapped. He hadn't really eaten for days. He didn't say anything else and he didn't resist.

Rachel stood by her front walkway and watched as the medics placed Jake on the stretcher, and as they wheeled him toward the vehicle. The ambulance drove off.

Thank God the children were still asleep and didn't see any of this...

She turned and visually took in the site of her farmhouse colonial home that was set back at an angle on the corner lot of her residential neighborhood. Rachel walked up the two steps to her front door, entered the living room and threw her body back onto the sofa. She must have dozed off for a few minutes, awakening only when she heard David in the kitchen.

16

He had never experienced any difficulty saying good-bye to anyone. But walking through the office door to the area where he had sat and observed her working not even forty-eight hours before was almost impossible. His small suitcase was dead weight. He didn't have much information to return home with, yet he couldn't afford to extend his stay.

He walked through the door and as he was about to sit, she caught his eye and waved him over. He waited patiently to the left of the counter allowing the woman with whom she was talking to finish. As soon as the woman turned to leave, Elena opened the side door to usher him in.

She was talking excitedly. "I had this brought to me by messenger. It is a listing of those who entered Auschwitz, but that's it. It doesn't have any other information. I've already checked it. Some of the names you asked about are here. None of the listings from DP camps had the names you wrote down. I'm sorry I don't have more to give you."

He stood trembling. Trembling about what he just heard. Trembling about his feelings toward this delicate young lady who stood before him. Her whole being exuded kindness and compassion. Yet, he was tugged by his guilt for having feelings toward a woman who did not share his faith, the faith for which his family members died.

He breathed deeply trying to gain control. Her scent was overpowering. She was looking at him intensely. Even though he was of average build, his suit jacket hung on his shoulders well. His coat was slung over his arm and a small suitcase was on the floor beside him.

"Can you stay?" she whispered, hesitantly.

"I wish I could." He allowed himself to hug her and be hugged by her. She felt comfort in his arms.

"Maybe we'll find out more. I'll keep researching. I will write if anything turns up. I told my father about your situation and even he suggested that you stay with us until we get more information."

"Thank you, but...Elena...I must return. I told you last night how I scrimped and saved to make this trip. I've already traveled to three cities and I only have a finite amount of vacation time and funds. This isn't easy for me. I have never, ever felt this way about anyone, Elena. You must believe me. But I must go home even though I want you with me. Allow me to hold out a little hope that I will work hard and save enough to be able to help you and your father. You really mean something to me."

She was trying hard not to cry aloud. She knew she had to get back to work. The tears rolled down her face, but she was silent. He gently kissed her moist cheek and mouthed good-bye. He placed the envelope with the sheets of information she had given to him inside his suit jacket pocket, lifted his suitcase and left the office.

17

It had been only three weeks since the last hospital visit and now Jake was back in the Emergency Room. Again Jake's sodium level was too low. The hiccups had returned.

Every day there were more tests, EEGs, CAT scans, x-rays, MRIs, and blood tests. And every day another specialist was added to the team, all the "ologists" who poked and prodded; with all the test results returning as negative. This was too bizarre to every specialist who looked at his medical record.

Somehow, through all the medical madness, Rachel sensed that she had to make necessary preparations to handle her uncle's personal business. His health continued to deteriorate. Rachel called the lawyer to prepare a Power of Attorney and a Will and with both in-hand, she went over to the hospital. At seven-thirty in the evening it was quiet on the ward. It took the lawyer some time explaining every detail to

Uncle Jake, but somehow he finally understood he could no longer procrastinate. The paperwork was completed bedside with hospital visitors as witnesses. Rachel read his eyes like a book. The emotion of the situation was overwhelming, very far from his coping mechanisms. The public persona that he had perfected over a lifetime was stripped away by some sort of insidious disease He looked toward Rachel as if pleading for help and, trying to suppress tears, blurted, "What do I have but you and the kids?" He had made his decisions and signed his name. Nothing more was ever mentioned about legal papers and after everyone left the room, Jake simply asked for the bedpan.

The ensuing weeks showed rapid signs of deterioration. Jake wasn't eating and he wasn't remembering. Not just forgetting. It was different. It was worse. He didn't remember incidents that happened. He didn't remember driving up to Connecticut to see the doctor. He didn't know where he was. He couldn't recall that he'd been in the hospital before. He was no longer able to process information. Repeatedly, he'd asked for Rachel's phone number and patiently, she would write it in very large numbers so he could easily see it. He took the piece of paper and tried to read it. Only he would hold it upside down.

At least he still recognized Rachel.

Jake's bills had to be paid and Rachel could no longer hold off. She was now completely responsible for her uncle's business affairs. As she handled each piece of mail, her uncle's life began to unfold.

She learned that Uncle Jake rented a storage area in a facility not too far from his apartment. It was a hot, humid, sticky, summer day and the air was stagnant and heavy as Rachel and her mom waited for the woman behind the service desk to assist. She cracked her gum as she searched the records for the box, called over a manager to review Rachel's fiduciary forms, and finally allowed the two upstairs accompanied by a worker to break the lock.

As the elevator opened on the sixth level, Rachel felt as if she couldn't breathe. They followed the signs posted on the aisles to find the storage number that belonged to Jake. There were no windows, or at least any that were visible. The area was dark, poorly lit by a few bare bulbs. There was no air. It felt as if there was only dust. It didn't take long before Rachel's head was spinning as she felt her heart pounding out of her chest, the most outrageous thoughts running through her head. She didn't really know Uncle Jake. It was as if she was peeling an onion and discovering layers upon layers of a personality. Who knew what was behind that storage door? Her mind was running wild. She had read too many mysteries. There could be a dead body in there! *Don't be ridiculous!* she told herself. *Be calm.* Perspiration was dripping from her forehead down to her eyes. Rachel pushed her glasses up to the bridge of her nose before they slipped off her face.

At last, the padlock was broken. A cloud of dislodged dust smacked Rachel's face as the storage door opened. She coughed uncontrollably. Rachel's mom stood by her side and reached in to sample some of the papers and books that had been stored there for ages. It, too, was all garbage; outdated textbooks and papers relating to Jake's teaching career. The bags within bags filled with books and papers were merely a subset of his apartment. Rachel tried not to cry yet again, but this time the tears were an expression of relief rather than sadness.

18

As the pasta boiled on the stove, Rachel was slicing a tomato when her mom interrupted, that familiar voice on the phone filled with a sense of urgency mixed with fatigue. Perhaps Rachel mistakenly confused geriatric depression with fatigue.

"Rachel!"

Now what? Rachel thought.

"I went to the bank today and had them drill open Jake's safety deposit box. You have a minute?" Rachel never had a minute to herself, but she had no choice but to listen. The lawyer had advised that Jake's things be removed from his bank safety deposit box. Mom had co-signing privileges for the box and, indeed, she exercised that privilege.

Mom described her experience discovering a wad of bonds—some war bonds—and stacks of one-hundred-dollar bonds. Envelopes stuffed with stock certificates.

"Rachel, I don't know what to do with this now."

Rachel released a nervous chuckle. She didn't know what to say and she was certainly surprised that such a significant investment was found, but what did she know about stocks and bonds? "Hang onto it and I'll pick it up and open a vault here."

"So how's Jake?" David asked during dinner.

"Same. No change. But Mom called." Rachel checked down the hall to make sure Abby and Adam were out of earshot before she told David what Mom found.

David closed the door to the office to use the phone privately. When he returned a few minutes later, he spoke firmly. "Rachel, we're going down to Mom's now."

"I can't. I'm too tired. What's the rush?" Rachel was finally sitting with her feet propped up on another kitchen chair sipping fresh coffee from a large mug. Her feet were throbbing and she did not want to go anywhere.

"We'll call Mom from the car." David was insistent.

"It can wait until tomorrow. Please!" Rachel was adamant.

"This is too important, Rachel, and you are responsible for this. I'm trying to help you. This way you won't have to drive alone again tomorrow."

"I'm really not happy about this. What exactly did the lawyer say?"

"That we get what Mom found and handle it here. Come on, Rach, let's go."

Rachel didn't have the strength to argue and put on her shoes.

"Abby!" Rachel called to the other room as she walked toward the den where the kids were watching T.V. "Abby, Daddy and I have to go out for an hour or so. Please make sure you and Adam do your homework. Call us on the car phone if you need anything. We'll keep it with us and please don't fight." Abby was distracted by the television and Rachel doubted she really heard everything she said.

It was 9:30 in the evening when Mom finally finished describing every detail of what happened at the bank. When she paused for a breath, Rachel didn't wait. "We've been advised to open a securities account and to change the names on the stocks and bonds so there are co-owners. Otherwise, it'll be an absolute mess should the worst happen."

Rachel's mom thought for a moment. "It makes sense. I don't have a problem with that. I'm still shocked at what I found. My eyes were popping out of my head as I inventoried everything. Look, here's the list. And I couldn't help but think about the times Jake and I supposedly spoke frankly about finances. He assured me all he had was a 401K and an IRA account. But look at all this! Did he know? Did he even realize…?"

Rachel placed all the stocks and bonds into a navy blue nylon bag and ran the zipper across the top. "Mom, let's not analyze Uncle Jake right now. I have to get home. Thanks for doing all this work. I'm not sure about anything and I'm certainly not knowledgeable about this stuff."

Rachel clutched the bag tightly even through she was safely seated in the car with the doors locked.

David and Rachel were still awake after midnight as they sat cross-legged on the floor in their den, the piles of stocks and bonds encircling them. They were taking inventory, alphabetizing and documenting the stocks, not knowing its worth, but having an idea that it was substantial.

"You know we'll have to go back into his apartment to make sure there aren't any more stocks or valuables kept there before you hire someone to clean up," David advised.

Rachel hadn't considered that. The emotional stress was taking its toll and David knew it. The thought of handling Jake's finances was an overwhelming responsibility for Rachel. David was trying to be logical and step her through all she had to do.

"I know you don't want to handle Uncle Jake's business matters, but you're the only one who can. That's why you have Power of Attorney."

Rachel followed her husband's advice and was at the bank doorstep when it opened the following morning. It didn't take long before the branch manager strolled over to introduce himself after eyeing the contents of Rachel's briefcase. Rachel had dressed for the part in a conservative business suit and sensible heels, and accordingly, the bank staff was extremely solicitous, attending to all of Rachel's requests. By the time she left the bank a few hours later, she knew the valuables were safe.

All the responsibilities came crashing down on Rachel like dominoes, one after another. Uncle Jake's medical needs, his finances, and the most monumental task of all—how to clean that apartment.

"You'll have to hire professionals. You can't do it yourself," David's voice echoed. Frustration mounted as Rachel tried to call different social agencies to get help. Finally David suggested calling a *private* waste management company.

"Genius. Now I know why I married you." Rachel lifted her head back to look up to his face as he stood behind her. His black hair was graying at the temples. His deep brown eyes behind small oval glasses were intense and kind at the same time.

Rachel studied the listings under "Sanitation Services" in the Yellow Pages, but found nothing. She then checked under the category "Garbage." Again, no listings. Under the topic "Waste Management" there were five or six. She called each; most of them only provided dumpsters. The last listing was it—a company that not only provided the dumpsters but also provided a crew to shovel out the mess! At that point, she didn't care how much it would cost. She had to start somewhere and scheduled it for Thursday, three days away.

Rachel and David returned to Jake's apartment the following evening, prepared with surgical masks and gloves. "You're not breathing in that dust. Wear them," David urged. Rachel's stomach felt uneasy, even a little queasy. Pausing before opening the apartment door, she fumbled with the keys long enough for David to take them from her and unlock the lock. Rachel just glared at him.

"You look through the pile of envelopes on the kitchen table and I'll get over to the desk in the bedroom," David instructed. He held Rachel's hand as she climbed over piles of paper, slipping on magazines. Nearly losing her balance she managed to get her footing on a small piece of solid floor by the kitchen where she started her search. She opened envelopes and checked for important papers, but she was very unsure about how she could distinguish what was important and what was not. Everything could be important. Anything could be garbage. What did she know about his life? She took some papers that looked like statements and stock dividend stubs, but otherwise, left everything intact.

"How're you doing?" She yelled to David.

"Come here. I think you'll want to see what I found."

"Easier said than done," she called back. She held her palms against the walls as she maneuvered the narrow hallway leading to the bedroom.

"Check out this bag," David said.

"I can't breathe." Rachel started to look through the brown envelopes in the paper grocery store bag stuffed in the plastic bag. The perspiration was dripping down her face and her glasses were foggy. But they read each other's eyes over the surgical masks after Rachel glanced at the bag's contents. It was yet another collection of stock certificates.

"David!..." Her coughing interrupted her speech. David turned to take out another envelope. "I'm glad we came down tonight before that waste management company starts to shovel this stuff."

Rachel took the envelope out of David's hand and shoved it back in the bag. David continued his search in the bedroom and through the desk and armoire. As she clutched the bag and climbed over the piles of papers back toward the front door she eyed another table in the living room.

"There's another table-like desk in the back of the living room, David. It's also stacked with envelopes and papers. I'm going to look through that now."

She maneuvered her way toward the desk. The dust was thick and her gloves were blackened. By balancing on top of the piles on the floor and holding on to the edge of the table, Rachel was fairly secure that she would not slip. She found copies of tax forms and copies of more stock certificates that she kept. Statements of various mutual fund and IRA accounts were all over the table. It was difficult to read them all to determine which were still active. There were accounts dating back twenty years. But what surprised Rachel most was that she had never seen statements with such large sums in the total column. If they were all active, did her uncle understand what he had? How did he amass all this? There were too many questions; too many things she didn't understand. As she stood by the table and stared at the papers, she thought of all the bizarre events that brought them there.

"Can we please get out of here?" she pleaded.

"In just a minute. Let me finish looking through some more of the stuff by the desk."

"David, I'm going out to the hall. I can't breathe. Please, let's go," she begged, her voice more insistent.

"Rachel, just a minute. Look at this!"

"David, I don't care anymore. Please—let's go!" She was impatient and just wanted to leave.

"Okay, I'm coming." David was carefully watching his footing as he came out of the bedroom and made his way toward the front door. He was holding a dusty box under his arm. Clutching a bag of envelopes and papers, Rachel walked out into the hall first and yanked the surgical mask off her face and removed the blackened gloves. She tossed them in the incinerator chute near the elevator. She stood back against the wall waiting for the elevator when her knees weakened and she slid down, completely exhausted. David came out to her, took the keys from her hand, and locked the door. He helped her stand up, completely supporting her body as she buried her head into his chest and cried. By the time the elevator came, the front of David's shirt was tear-stained.

"I'm sorry this is so difficult for you. You have to face these realities. Uncle Jake is very sick. I saw Dr. Katzen at the pool this morning and he told me he didn't think it looked good. You just don't have all these bizarre symptoms without considering a tumor. I really love Uncle Jake, too. I'm sorry, Rachel."

David continued, "I found some things you're going to want to see..."

19

The weeks passed and it was inevitable that Rachel hear the blunt truth from the doctor.

"He's dying, Rachel. He's getting worse and it is undiagnosed so we can't even help him get better. It's just as frustrating for us as it is for you."

"Why can't you find out what's wrong? After all these tests?!" Rachel raised her voice.

"I've seen incidences where tests are conducted over three months before we have a diagnosis."

"Are we dealing with a cancer?" Rachel was so afraid to say the word. Her dad had died of cancer.

"No one is sure. But it looks that way. I've brought in an oncologist. We're going to have to be very aggressive in testing. I'm also working with a surgeon so we can schedule a few biopsies."

"Have you explained all this to him?"

"Yes. We've explained it. I've been in there alone and I've been in there with the surgeon. But Jake doesn't remember. And he'll ask the same question over and over and over." The doctor went on. "You do know that he refused a test today. We are forced into a position where we are going to have to ask you for your consent since he no longer seems capable of making decisions for himself."

"Will he ever be able to go back to his apartment again?"

"No." The doctor's reply was simple and direct. "The social worker will give you information on options for long-term care facilities. It's time you face it, Rachel," the doctor advised, "you'll have to handle *all* his affairs now including making all the decisions."

20

December 4, 1949

My dear Jake,

It was so nice to hear from you and hear that your family is fine. Father is doing fairly well although the winters hit him harder each year. We both appreciate your generous gift. It will help us fix the heating in the house, which, in turn, will help my father feel much more comfortable. You have a heart of gold.

Congratulations on your brother's marriage. I'm sure your family is delighted to have a happy occasion to celebrate.

I do miss you and think of you often. I am always so happy to receive your letters and news about you. Sometimes, during my days at the office, I get very depressed. I've been hearing more and more about all sorts of horrors that happened during the war. The news and information about what really transpired only gets worse. I'm afraid to continually talk to Father about it because it will only upset him more, yet I need to be able to talk to someone. How can we, as fellow humans, socially and emotionally cope with what happened? How can we live with ourselves?

I feel as if I'm hearing and learning too much about it just because of where I work. Most of my neighbors have heard some things but don't seem to be bothered by it. They attribute much of what they hear to rumors. The newspapers claim to be "protecting their readers" until they can provide the real truth. The real truth they have to figure out is how to come to terms with all this and how the world perceives their country. I can see the difference in how your newspapers are covering the aftermath of the war. At least they are dealing with it.

I so wish I were closer to you to talk and to make some sense of this madness.

Take care of yourself, Jake.

Love,
Elena

P.S. I promise to read all the books you sent before my next letter!

21

Handling all the calls became a full time job. Jake's friends called frequently, wanting up-to-date information. Rachel tried to be patient, but they had the same difficulty as she not having answers. Some were so determined they even tried calling the doctor directly or tried to get information from the hospital nurses. Rachel had prepared for that and instructed that all calls were to be referred to her. Letters, postcards, and Get Well cards began to fill her mailbox. Most included very nice notes and concerned sentiments. A few were surprisingly nasty, insinuating that Rachel wasn't doing enough or doing the best for Jake; that she should transfer him to the Westchester hospital. *Who do they think they are? They haven't come to visit Uncle Jake once! Would they take care of Jake?* One friend in particular was especially tenacious.

The nurse walked briskly into Jake's hospital room. She was quite agitated. "A Dr. Stanvic is on the phone demanding information. I don't know any Dr. Stanvic and I'm not allowed to give her any information!" She placed her hands defiantly on her hips.

Mom was visiting at the time and responded to the nurse. "I'll take the call." Although the pain in her knee bothered her, she walked with determination to the phone at the nursing station.

"Are you a medical doctor or a Ph.D.?" Mom asked the caller.

"A Ph.D." she replied. "In Humanities."

"A friend!" Mom later told Rachel, "The nerve! Getting a nurse flustered by using her title improperly. If this dame felt she couldn't get enough information about Jake by phone, why hasn't she visited him? He's certainly been in the hospital long enough! Some friend!"

Rachel made a mental note of the incident.

Indeed, Elizabeth was the only friend who did come to visit Jake weekly. She had never learned to drive and depended on getting a ride from a friend—her little, fat, friend—as she referred to him. He drove Elizabeth from Long Island to the Connecticut hospital every week. *Strange relationships,* Rachel thought as she observed him waiting; patiently sitting for hours in front of the hospital building taking in the sun, while Elizabeth visited with Jake.

Jake was all smiles during Elizabeth's visits. He laughed. They talked. She brought him a beautiful plant. She tried to get him to eat. No success.

The hospital coffee shop was usually quiet when Elizabeth joined Rachel for a cup of coffee. Without any family, this must be horribly difficult for her,

Rachel thought. Elizabeth—always Elizabeth, never Liz or Beth—was so very dependent on Jake, having been his companion for so many years. She told Rachel that she had wanted Jake to sign her Living Will and other medical and legal forms but Jake never took that final step of trust and intimacy. Elizabeth accepted that along with all his other eccentricities.

In her soft British accent, she'd repeat herself. "But I don't understand! How can the doctors not know? You can't keep poking and bothering the man with tests! That's exhausting for him, too!"

The two spoke of his apartment. The sadness was easily read in her soft blue-gray eyes. "Don't you find it odd that he would be so meticulous with things in *my* apartment? He would even criticize me if something was out of place!" Elizabeth added. As time went on, there were plenty of odd things that kept surfacing…

22

Rachel was red in the face, totally enraged at the superintendent of the building, "You're useless! I can't believe you won't help me! You are absolutely heartless!"

She stood there alone, at 8:15 in the morning, in the middle of the lobby of the apartment building, screaming at a man who hardly spoke a word of English. He stomped off into his hole of a workshop and she stomped off through the front glass doors of the building to phone the managing agent.

Voice mail. "Al, this is Rachel. I'm at the building and I'm not getting any cooperation whatsoever from Tony. You specifically assured me that he would arrange a space in front of the building for the dumpster. Tony told me he couldn't do that. You know, I'm paying a hefty price to get this apartment cleaned up. I could've easily walked away from all this and left this for you guys to worry about." She took a breath. “Call me immediately on my cell phone or at the apartment.” Rachel went upstairs to the apartment knowing that nothing in this situation was ever going to be easy.

Rachel’s closest friend, Debra had come to help. She was already in the apartment and cleared some papers off the right side of the sofa to create what she called “Command Central.” They were prepared.

Finally, the buzzer rang from downstairs. The waste management crew had arrived. The black and dark green garbage barrels were wheeled off the elevator and into the hallway until a path could be cleared within the apartment. Shovels were brought upstairs by other workers. And then the team began working as the assembly line went into action. Five men shoveled the papers from the front hallway and shoved them into the barrels. Three other men then dragged the barrels into the elevator and brought them downstairs. Four men were passing the barrels up the street like a relay race to the dumpster. Two more men dumped the garbage into the dumpster and returned the barrels to the men who passed the barrels back to the building. It was as if it was all orchestrated to music. It followed a consistent, quick rhythm in an effort to clear out a one-bedroom apartment.

Debra and Rachel sifted through papers and books and other supplies that could be kept, always on the lookout for any valuables. None of the cartons could be opened until there was room to walk within the apartment. Rachel worked at the cherry wood trestle table toward the rear of the living room, looking through stacks of papers. There were boxes of books and cartons covered in inches of dust around her feet.

Learning from past experience, Rachel insisted they wear the light blue surgical masks and rubber surgical gloves brought from David's dental office. David's point was accurate—the apartment was a health risk. They needed to get some air into the apartment. Debra reached over and struggled to open the window from the bottom, then used a Webster's dictionary to prop it and hold it in place. Rachel found at least four fans, but only two worked. They plugged them in toward the front of the apartment and dust was blown throughout. Eventually the fans created some air movement in the stifling hot apartment.

"Hello?" The familiar voice bellowed from the hallway.

"Hi, Mom. Pull up a corner and look through stuff."

"Here, why doesn't your mom use this chair to sit in the hall? We can pass her some of these cartons and she can start to look through them," Debra suggested as she lifted the folding chair and handed it to one of the crew members in the hall.

It was astute of Debra to set up Mom with a concrete task. Rachel didn't want to be distracted and she didn't want to move from where she was standing. Just climbing back over the piles toward the front door was too much of a chore for her at that point.

Rachel continued to sift through papers and Debra organized the piles on the sofa. The right side was reserved for those items worth saving and Rachel was surprised to see the pile growing. Boxes of rubber bands, unopened packages of loose-leaf paper, note pads, pens, calculators, and light bulbs were mixed in the pile with statements of mutual funds, IRAs, and copies of stock certificates.

The shoveling continued. The work crew handed cartons out to Mom who sat on a metal folding chair in the hallway. She was going through the boxes and found old pocketbooks belonging to Jake's mother and aunt. Uncle Jake had never unpacked anything from Rachel's grandparents' apartment or her great aunt's apartment. Each old, ratty-looking pocketbook typically contained a five-dollar bill, a small rectangular mirror, a makeup compact, comb, and crumpled Kleenex.

Whatever Rachel considered unimportant, she tossed on the floor to be shoveled out. Otherwise, it was handed to Debra who filled clean cartons with items and papers to be kept. Sometime in the late morning, they began to open cartons in an attempt to clear the front hall before noon. One of the men bent down to help Rachel unpack and lifted out a pair of tarnished silver candlesticks.

"Bubby's candlesticks! We finally found them!" Rachel's voice exuded an excitement for the first time in months. On examination, she saw that a leg was broken off one of the candlesticks and the set was in disrepair. She didn't mind, though, she had located the one item she had been asking for since she was a bride. And asked for again when her daughter became a Bat Mitzvah. This was the very pair Rachel's grandmother had brought with her from Eastern Europe over seventy years ago. Rachel remained still, frozen, crouched over the carton, tightly holding them until Debra reached over and took them from her hands. Sensing Rachel's reluctance to release them from her grip, she assured Rachel, "I'll wrap them carefully for you. You can take them home in this bag later." Debra motioned to the clean bag she set aside for them.

Rachel regained her composure. "Thanks." She paused. "I think we should break for lunch soon." She called out to Mom. "How're you doing there? Ready to take a break?"

"How about going over to Greenery's? It's just down the block," she called back. "And there's a pizza place across from it so you can bring back some pizza for the men."

The surgical mask and gloves were thrown to the floor as they left. Despite the humidity, Rachel appreciated being able to breathe. The emotional intensity of sifting through Jake's papers and possessions was so great, Rachel had felt as if she had been holding her breath for hours.

"I just can't come to grips with all this. We had some idea, but never in a million years…and Dad would never ask…he would never intrude in his brother's life…" Mom rambled through lunch. "It's not as if we didn't talk about things…including financial matters. But he never told me about his extra health insurance from the retirement association. You'd think he'd share some of that information with me. After all, I was trying to help him get that catastrophic insurance!"

"Let me tell you about the specials of the day," the waitress interrupted.

"That's okay," Rachel answered. "We know what we want. Two tuna sandwiches on rye and one vegetable lasagna, two Diet Cokes with lemon and one regular coffee with milk, please. Thanks." The waitress scribbled the order and walked toward the kitchen.

"Mom, I understand. But I'm feeling awful right now. I'm feeling guilty for going through his things and having his house cleaned up. I'm just hoping he'll be able to come home with a nurse or something. The doctors don't think he'll ever be able to come back."

"My father went through this with my uncle," Debra reminisced. I was a small girl at the time, but I remember having to sit on the stoop outside his building. I was never allowed to go into my uncle's apartment. By the time I saw it, my parents had already cleaned out a substantial amount of stuff. But my uncle did at least have a small space at his kitchen table to eat something or to have a cup of coffee."

The waitress returned with the drinks.

Rachel's mom talked incessantly about Jake. Rachel tried to tune it out but snippets of the chatter seeped in, "…The more I learn about this, the sicker I feel, although I've heard this is not that uncommon. There was a famous story years ago about the Collier brothers…two brothers who were found dead in their house on piles of garbage…"

Lunch was placed on the table.

"Can we change the subject *please*?" It was obvious that Rachel was impatient and irritable. "I'd like to eat. As it is I feel skuzzy…" She didn't want to talk about anything at that point. The conversation turned to the mundane and Rachel vaguely remembered actually having a laugh during lunch.

Less than an hour later they were back at the apartment with three boxes of pizzas and a bag filled with soda cans for the crew. Everyone worked non-stop until 3:30 in the afternoon, clearing out as much as possible. They raked piles of papers and garbage, shoveled and dumped. The crew, with Rachel's guidance, moved efficiently from one area to the next. Occasionally someone called out a question.

Bankbooks were found, old tax returns, old business checks and ledgers from Rachel's great aunt's lingerie stores in Brooklyn. Familiar handwriting surrounded Rachel—the written remains of two generations of family all gone—her grandparents, great aunt and uncle, and father. Childhood memories flashed in her mind. It was getting too difficult to be objective. Rachel kept pausing to examine papers and read old greeting cards, lingering longest over old photographs. Photographs, similar to those David discovered in a dusty box a few days earlier, along with old immigration papers and visas.

Photographs. Younger versions of faces she once knew as she was growing up. Faces of generations past of people she did not recognize. Family… friends … who once lived in the shtetls of Europe. Family who did not survive the concentration camps of World War II. She was determined to find out who these people were. Some photographs were mounted on postcards with messages on the back—messages in Yiddish, messages in Polish…Notes she didn't understand. A burning desire would remain with her—a craving to have all these notes and boxes of letters translated from Yiddish. She had to do it. She had to do it before the ink faded completely and the paper crumbled to the touch.

At 3:15 the crew called it quits. Debra called out from the bedroom; "I'll come to a stopping point soon.

I'm just putting stuff on the bed I think you'd want to save or take a look at another time."

Another time. Rachel hadn't thought about returning to this apartment again. Looking around, she knew the waste management crew had to return to finish clearing out the apartment. But it would be up to Rachel to endure sifting through the rest of the items to determine what might be worth saving. Is this where the road to life leads? Rachel's own life was in havoc, worrying about Uncle Jake and how to manage his life.

23

June 14, 1954

My dear Jake,

Thank you for your letters, gifts and your kindness. Although it has been difficult for me since Father died, and God forgive me for adding this, it has been a bit of a relief, too. Your generosity has helped me go on without worrying about losing pay for not going to the office. Even though people have been very kind to me, at the office and otherwise, I feel negligent staying at home so much. But I have to get Father's affairs in order and I have to move on with my life. I guess as people mature and go through different stages, they learn what realities are and the priorities in life. Apparently, many had remembered things I did for them or said to them during their difficult times and they feel they must reciprocate. Honestly, Jake, I don't even remember that I've ever done anything special.

During my weaker moments, I curl up with one of the books you've sent over the past years and I spend time reading the inscriptions you've carefully worded for me. Your words bring me great comfort. I, too, hope you are enjoying your work and your life.

I was so excited to hear about the birth of your niece! My heartfelt congratulations! Your parents must be so happy that the family is growing again. There is nothing quite like having a baby in a family to bring smiles to faces and to make everyone feel young again. Sight unseen, I know you will spoil that little girl, Jake, and I imagine you will enjoy every minute of it. Inside, I laugh at my images of you playing with her.

How can I ever forget the day we spent together and how patient and sweet you were to the children by the fountain! The few minutes of playing "hit the coin" with the rubber ball brought back childish sparkles in their eyes; the children's eyes that had matured too fast because of war; eyes that saw too much tragedy in life. Eyes transformed back to life even for a few fanciful minutes. I know you are wonderful with children and I will continue to get much pleasure from my thoughts of you with the baby.

I've heard that most new parents purchase a camera. Perhaps you can send a picture of yourself with baby Cheryl. I would like that very much. Cheryl is such a pretty name. I have learned that usually Jewish families name their children after deceased relatives. Should I venture a guess that she was named after your grandmother?

Love,
Elena

24

Rachel's family was no longer a separate entity. It seemed as if Jake's life overtook their life; their mailbox was overstuffed with mail that was being forwarded from Jake's address. Rachel tackled the monumental task of opening his envelopes, paying his bills, reviewing business records and balancing his checkbook.

A review of a VISA bill raised her brow. *This must be a mistake*, she thought. A charge from a cosmetic surgery center in New York was posted on a date Jake was in the hospital. *Odd, but mistakes happen*, she thought.

Dutifully, she contacted the credit card company for the necessary form to contest the charge and called the Cosmetic Surgery Center. No, they didn't have Jake's name, date of birth, or Social Security number in their database. Maybe they were off a digit on the credit card number.

The calls from Jake's friends eventually subsided, with the exception of Elizabeth and Dr. Tanya Stanvic, the *friend* who had called the nursing station. Stanvic called Rachel to introduce herself as a friend of Jake's. It wasn't long before Rachel took a disliking to her; she was unusually insistent, demanding to know what the doctors were doing for him, what the diagnosis was, where he was and why he couldn't talk on the phone. As she prodded for information, Rachel graciously and successfully skirted a lot of the questions. It wasn't that difficult, truthfully, since she did not have a lot of answers.

"It's too bad you have to go through this, Rachel, at such a young age." Tanya spoke with a heavy, European accent. "Jake has spoken to me about you and the kids. He adores your children. I hear about them all the time."

"Yes, I know how he feels about my kids." Rachel wanted to change the subject back to her. "Where do *you* know Jake from?"

"Oh, I met him through the Shakespeare Club in New York. He's a very kind and generous man."

"Why haven't you come to Connecticut to visit with him? He'd like that."

"I don't have a car and I'd need to get a ride. I'd have to figure it out," she responded.

Yet another one of Jake's friends who would not visit; who would give a lame excuse as to why she couldn't visit her "dear friend" Jake. Rachel's opinion of Jake's friends changed for the worse. They were all lazy and self-centered.

25

Abby and Adam were waiting in front of the school with their backpacks slung over their shoulders, slightly bent from the weight of their books. Rachel drove up the circular driveway to pick them up early so they could visit Uncle Jake. She didn't know she picked a bad day for the children to visit, especially when the initial greeting from Uncle Jake seemed normal. A few minutes into the visit though, Jake became frighteningly incoherent.

"Well, hello!" Uncle Jake greeted as they approached his bed.

"Hi! How are you feeling today?" Rachel was glad he sounded so upbeat.

"Okay, okay. Better than Coney Island," he responded.

Rachel saw Adam look over toward Abby. "Huh?" he mouthed to her. Rachel hadn't anticipated the possibility of Jake being mentally impaired so she had not prepared the children.

"Hey…look who is here with me, Jake," Rachel continued normally.

"Hey…yeah…" Uncle Jake's eyes did not light up as they usually did when he saw the children. He didn't seem to know them.

"Remember Adam's ball game?" Rachel prompted.

"Yeah, yeah. How's baseball?"

Adam just stood as his body swayed slightly. His eyes peered from under the brim of his Yankees cap as he looked toward his mom hesitatingly and then toward his sister. "Good," he replied meekly.

"Jake, remember this young la." Before Rachel could finish the word *lady,* Jake interrupted.

"Yeah! That's your good friend from next door."

Rachel's pre-teen daughter was about to fall apart. Abby was a very emotionally sensitive girl and her body language clearly demonstrated how hurt she was. She tried with every ounce of strength in her petite body to hold back tears of disappointment and hurt.

"Jake, you know Abby. You were at her Bat Mitzvah a few months ago."

"Abby. Yes. E…v…y…a…" He tried to spell her name. Abby, completely bewildered, was about to correct him, but Rachel quickly glanced at the two children and said, "Yes. That's it."

His mental processes had deteriorated. Connections between thoughts were short-circuiting, becoming totally random. His short-term memory was non-existent. Abby walked out of the room so no one would see her cry. Adam walked out after her a few minutes later. Rachel was about to follow them when Jake motioned to her.

"Go outside and walk back in slowly. Shh! Go ahead!" he insisted.

Humoring him, she did what he said.

"Now listen to how quietly and softly they chew," Jake said.

What is he talking about? Rachel was unqualified to know how to respond.

Jake looked around and mumbled something disjointedly.

"Where are you, Uncle Jake?" Rachel asked.

"East Cuba…East New York…" Jakes eyes seemed glassy, shallow, without any rational substance behind them.

The kids returned to the room. They were both upset that Uncle Jake didn't know them and that he wasn't making any sense. Always curious, Adam reached for the clipboard hanging from the foot of the bed.

"No, Adam. Leave it alone!" Rachel scolded.

"You better listen to the ship." Jake continued to ramble. "I was in this play for my friend. I have to get to the rehearsal." He tried to sit up to get out of bed.

"Jake, they canceled the rehearsal, because it's raining." Rachel tried to think quickly to appease him. He couldn't possibly get out of bed.

"They did? A funny thing though. This play…whenever anything happened to my character, I really felt it happening to me."

Jake tried to get up from the bed again. "Why are they keeping me here? It's Friday. I have to go. I have to pick up my car."

Rachel turned to Abby. “Quick, go get a nurse.” Abby obeyed and ran out of the room.

The nurse got Jake back into bed. She turned to Rachel, somewhat frustrated. “You know he tried to get out of bed three times today and peed on the floor.” Rachel had hoped the children weren’t nearby. She didn’t need them watching the nurse put a lead vest on Jake as a restraint.

Rachel called the children in just to say good-bye to their great uncle and they quickly left. Abigail looked traumatized. Adam was too young to understand. Rachel took each by the hand and led them through the hospital halls to another wing on the third floor. There, the three of them stood, looking through the glass in the nursery at newborn babies. Rachel was a little more relaxed now as she tried to create a positive diversion for her children.

“They’re so tiny!” Adam exclaimed.

“Yes, honey, and you were that size once, too. But much, much cuter.” Rachel held him close.

“Hey! What about me?” Abigail chimed.

“You?” Rachel smiled at her. “You were the most adorable *girl* the nurses ever saw!”

Abigail began to smile a little. At twelve years old, she was almost her mother’s height. Rachel felt her daughter’s long chestnut brown hair brush against her cheek when Abby rested her head on her shoulder. Rachel put her arms around the children and held them close. She felt her son’s eyelashes tickle her other cheek. Slowly, she guided them toward the elevator. “Let’s go. We can stop for a snack on the way out.” Rachel prayed she had eased their distress after their painful visit with Uncle Jake.

The days turned into weeks and Uncle Jake's health deteriorated rapidly. The feeding tube, inserted directly into his stomach, marked the beginning of the end. The dementia was the most difficult to bear, as Rachel watched a charming, modest, gentleman degenerate to a confused and crude, agitated ghost of a man. He would throw his blanket off to proudly display the feeding tube, a plastic, milky snake that had been surgically attached to his body. Rachel would casually lift the blanket to cover his bony, thin, naked body, straining to retain some poise with every ounce of strength she had, masking her repulsion. A nurse with a heavy Scottish accent would check in and speak to Jake about his past, "so he won't become agitated," she explained.

"Notice how his speech and memory are that much clearer the further back you go," the nurse commented astutely. She faced Jake but continued to talk to Rachel. "Yes, he had quite a journey last night. He and his roommate took a drive north up the Palisades and had a grand ol' time." Her facial expression and gestures indicated that Jake had totally lost his mind. But Uncle Jake chuckled as the nurse described how he behaved and what he had said. The nurse turned to Rachel, "It may be the cortisone the doctors are giving him—the anti-inflammatory—to reduce his fevers."

"Fevers?" The doctor hadn't told Rachel that Jake was running fever.

"He's been having unexplained fevers," the nurse continued. "Sometimes the cortisone can cause the 'loonies.'" Facing Jake, smiling, she added, "But we're taking good care o' you now, Jake. Right?" Jake smiled back.

26

August 13, 1979

My dear Jake,

You have always been so wonderful to me over the years. As the years have passed, I have often had tears of gratitude when I have a quiet moment to think of you.

Long ago, but sometimes it seems like yesterday, in 1958, when I wrote you that I was marrying Henri, my heart was breaking. I heard your voice in your letters and your words as you supported me through difficult times and decisions. Henri is a good man and I've been trying to care for him now in the same way he's cared for me. He was so patient and worked so hard to gain my affections. But, still, it's hard for me. And now, watching him succumb to this horrible disease is so disheartening. He tries so to be courageous and I try to be a source of comfort to him. You would have liked him, Jake. He, too, has an unquenchable thirst for knowledge.

So what are we doing with this quest for knowledge? It didn't save my father and it isn't saving Henri either. Most importantly, it hasn't helped us be together.

Forgive my foolish ramblings. I'm tired, Jake, and my mind, my memories, can't shake your warmth, can never shake you. I am very blessed that you are a part of my life.

Love,
Elena

27

New Orleans. The Big Easy. You could hear jazz wherever you walked. Rachel had about six hours all to herself to discover a city far away from her responsibilities. David had been concerned that the emotional strain Rachel had been experiencing at home was too great for her to handle. It had affected Rachel's entire personality and when it began to interfere with their relationship, David insisted that his wife join him while he attended a dental conference out-of-town. The change of venue left Rachel time to go out alone, without any demands, to be totally spontaneous. She felt an immense sense of freedom, an enormous burden lifted from her shoulders—albeit, only temporarily.

She dressed quickly in a pair of khaki green shorts and a white t-shirt, slipped on a black canvas backpack and went down to the concierge desk to find out about day tours. The trolley tour seemed ideal, she could get on and off at different stops for one fare. Bourbon Street, the French Quarter, Jazz and Mardi Gras, the famous above ground cemeteries—the aura of a city that inspired so many writers and stimulated imaginations with stories of vampires.

The stifling heat and humidity did not deter Rachel even though her glasses fogged and she felt as if she had walked into a steam bath. Very few pedestrians were about; air conditioned buildings were preferred. Yet nothing was going to stop her from having a day to wander aimlessly as she pleased. There was a renewed bounce in her step, revealing how much she needed a mental health day.

Rachel was glad when the trolley came along within ten minutes. She had mapped out her day as the tour guide described the sites and the stops. She got off at the Old U.S. Mint, examined the artwork on the authentic confederate money and carefully selected a souvenir for David, a true Civil War buff. She found her way through the French Quarter to Royal Street stopping in boutiques, trying on clothes and treating herself to a special brunch at Brennan's. As she sipped a Mimosa and nibbled on some fresh bread she took the time to delight in her anonymity, totally free from any sense of duty, treating herself in a manner to which she could easily become accustomed. She felt fabulous.

The two gentlemen at the next table were speaking rather loudly. At first Rachel found the conversation interesting, but after a while it became intrusive. Rachel yearned for quiet, to concentrate on her own thoughts—fantasizing of easier times, of traveling the world, of escaping the difficulties of day-to-day realities…

The waiter set an omelet before her with sliced fruits to its side in a floral design. She savored the taste. She seemed surprised that she was so hungry but then realized it was already one o'clock and she hadn't had anything to eat all day. The aches in her feet eventually subsided. Laden down with some additional packages, Rachel planned to continue down Royal Street to the next trolley stop to finish the tour and head back to the hotel.

The trolley rocked gently as it rode through the various neighborhoods of New Orleans, passed antebellum mansions and above ground cemeteries. The combination of the heat, the walking and touring tired Rachel, but it was a good tired. She opened the door to the hotel room and realized that David had not yet returned. The message indicator light on the phone was blinking.

Rachel peeled off her wet clothes, quickly showered, and dressed in some clean, dry shorts and shirt. She took a coke and some ice from the vending machine down the hall.

The bed was comfortable; Rachel propped some pillows behind her back to sit up, took a pencil and pad in hand and readied herself to listen to the phone messages. Cheryl's voice was totally unexpected. "*My sister called!? Why is she even calling me and how did she track me down here?*" Rachel thought. Rachel was curious and angry, mostly furious that her fantasy day was ruined. Her sense of calm immediately transformed into agitation. Rachel called home.

“I made a serious mistake,” Mom began. “I should have picked up the phone and hung up on her. Instead, I refused to pick up. Adam didn’t understand. He’s too young and I know in his own way he was trying to help. He wants to speak with you now.”

“Hi, Adam. How’s it going with…”

The little boy interrupted. “Mom, let me tell you what happened. Cheryl called and told me it was an emergency. She had to get in touch with you. I didn’t have your number, Grandma did. But she wouldn’t pick up! I told her it was an emergency, but she wouldn’t talk to her. Finally, I got the number and called her back. We talked a lot about different things, mostly about the Yankees. I didn’t know she knew about that stuff…”

“You did fine, Adam. Don’t worry about it. There are some things I’ll try to explain to you later.”

“No, tell me now,” Again, Adam persisted.

“Now is not the time. Where is your sister? Put her on the phone.”

“No, please tell me now.” He wouldn’t give up.

“Adam.” Rachel was impatient and certainly did not have the strength for his defiance long distance. “Be good and put your sister on the phone. Come on, Grandma needs your help and lots of love.”

His voice softened. “Okay, bye. But when will you be home?”

“Sunday night.”

“Okay, bye.” Rachel heard him scream “Ab-by!”.

Abby picked up fairly quickly. “Hi. How is everything going, Abby?”

“You heard what happened when Cheryl called?” she asked.

"Yeah, yeah. I heard the whole story. I can't imagine what is so important with her, but I'll give her a call. Just take care. I'll see you in a day and a half. I love you. Take care of your brother."

"Love you, too, Mommy. You better talk to Grandma before you call Cheryl. She's really upset."

"Okay, sweetheart."

"Bye. Here's Grandma again."

Now Rachel was left in a position to mother her mother. Emotions ran deep. Cheryl hadn't spoken to Mom for over fifteen years. Nearly twenty years ago, Cheryl had instructed Rachel not to call *her,* she would call Rachel. Years went by and Cheryl never called. The sisters never shared any significant life events together.

Cheryl was the estranged relative, yet, for some unexplainable reason, Rachel had felt some obligation to inform her sister about Uncle Jake's illness. That always perplexed Rachel especially because she harbored such anger against her sister for not visiting Dad before he died. It is such a waste of emotional energy and time trying to deal with Cheryl's childishness.

Cheryl's point of view, of course, was vastly different. After all, no one lived through what *she* had to endure growing up. But at forty-five, it was time she let go of her childhood problems and see her parents as human beings who make mistakes. Rachel's mind wandered, dreaming of finally telling off her older sister. "You are far too old to act like a stubborn child who thinks no one understands you. How can you be so brilliant and yet so emotionally immature?!"

Rachel was lost in thought deciding whether to call her sister in Cleveland. Unaware of the clicking of the door lock, Rachel was rather surprised to see David and the puzzled look on his face.

"How was your day?" David asked gently.

"Oh, great…until I returned here and I heard the messages. Cheryl called."

David didn't display any surprise. "I know. I heard the message when I came up during the lunch break and I've already called her."

"You what?!" Rachel's voice was raised.

"I spoke to her already," he repeated patiently. "She wanted to make plane reservations to come east to see Uncle Jake and she wanted to know if a week from Friday was okay with us. She had to pay for the tickets today in order to get the cheaper airfare."

"Why did you call her before speaking with me?!" Rachel was enraged; she could feel her face turning red.

David looked at his wife in disbelief. "Why are you so upset? Why are you raising your voice to me? I told her we wouldn't be around that weekend. But she was welcome anytime. I thought I was being hospitable to your family—to *your* sister."

"David, you know how I feel about *her!* She's never been around to help…never been around, period! And now she wants to breeze in whenever *she* feels like it?! And to top it off, she got Adam upset claiming it's an *emergency*—that she had to get in touch with us? What kind of emergency? She can easily afford to spend a little more on a ticket! So what if she doesn't get an immediate answer? Besides, what difference does it make if we're in town or not?" She was raising her voice to David again.

"I don't see what the big deal is. She wants to see Uncle Jake and she thought she'd get to see us."

"Bullshit!" Rachel pounded the bed. She was furious David couldn't see Cheryl's motives. "She wants me around because she can't handle anything emotional! Why do you think I'm taking care of everything and she hasn't helped at all? I don't want her in my house. I don't want her accidentally seeing any of Jake's business papers or anything we've brought back from his apartment. She hasn't been a part of any of our lives for years. Now is not the time for her to start. My being home and available for *her* should not be the determining factor as to whether or not she wants to see her uncle! I don't have to be around just because it's *convenient* for Cheryl. And I'll take my time calling her back. So she'll have to pay a little more for a ticket. It's not an emergency—even though *she* perceives it as such. Who is she to upset my children…?"

David just stood silently as Rachel sat back on the bed and tried to regain her self-control. "David, I'm sorry I'm yelling. You don't understand. It's just so frustrating. Here we are, away from it all—or so I thought—and then I have to deal with all this Cheryl nonsense. What happened to a calm weekend away? And my day had been so great up until now."

As David unbuttoned his shirt and rummaged through his suitcase for clothes, he answered. "Don't make such a big deal about everything. Just relax while I get changed and then we'll go downstairs for some dinner."

David showered and changed while Rachel took the time to make obligatory calls. The hospital nurse informed her that Uncle Jake was being moved to the nursing home while waiting for the results of the biopsies, and, of course, Mom was still upset about Cheryl.

The New Orleans weekend was marred; nevertheless, David tried to make the trip as pleasant as possible. He tired of hearing Rachel analyze, reanalyze and second-guess everything that was happening at home, obsessing over innocuous pieces of conversations, but his compassion constrained him from interrupting. Together, though, they strolled through the air-conditioned Riverwalk mall, ducking into stores and soaking in the flavors of the city. It was good to get away, but was it really worth it knowing what was waiting for them at home? It was an unspoken understanding; David and Rachel needed time to be together, to be a couple again and to focus on each other—even if it was only for forty-eight hours. David put his arm around his wife's shoulder; Rachel took a deep breath and melted under his embrace.

28

The ad was published in the Sunday Metropolitan section of the Times, November 3, 1985. The ad was in 8-point type; the size was no different from the rest. It was simple, but unusual copy.

In search of Jake Kessler,

friend of Elena Kranz since 1947. Urgent. Phone 212-691-0020.

His heart skipped a beat. She's in New York? A New York City number? All these years...

He was standing with his coat on while reading the newspaper in a friend's apartment. He was waiting for the rest of the book club members to arrive. He had just finished showing off the photo of his newborn grandniece, describing her tiny features and intelligent eyes. His eyes shone and his big smile displayed a sense of pride, similar to that of a first-time grandpa.

He paused a long time, staring at the ad. He was careful not to display any type of emotion. "May I take this section of the paper with me?" he asked the hostess. "Sure, Jake." It was not an unusual request. Jake often asked to keep parts of the newspaper.

Concentration eluded him. The book club members greeted each other. They'd been friends for over twenty-five years, meeting at each other's houses every month. He could not focus on anything anyone said. The hour and a half passed slowly. He begged off coffee and cake and excused himself earlier than usual. Everything was automatic: his drive home, parking the car, entering his apartment.

He settled on his bed and stared at the phone for what seemed an eternity. It had been an eternity since he'd heard her voice, sensed her presence, felt her tender body. He dialed the number and let the phone ring four times. Just as he was about to hang up an unrecognizable voice spoke in perfect English.

"Hello?"

"Hello. I saw the ad in the Times about Elena looking for a Jake Kessler?"

"Yes. I am looking for Mr. Kessler on behalf of Elena."

His heart sank. Why, after all these years, would he have expected to speak directly with Elena?

"I am Jake Kessler," he responded.

"I am so relieved to have found you! Can we meet? I have some correspondence from Elena for you and I need to talk to you."

"Who are you?"

"Marguerite, a long-time friend of Elena. We were neighbors for many years. I can't go into any more detail. I'd much rather speak in person."

"That's fine. Where would you like to meet?"

"How about the coffee shop at the Museum of Modern Art? Say 11:30, before the lunch rush hour."

"Okay. How will I know you?"

"Oh please forgive me. I am about 5'2" with short, blonde hair. I'll wear a navy blue suit, if that helps you."

"I'll be wearing a dark tan overcoat. Usually, I'm carrying a newspaper under my arm."

She laughed. "So I surmised. I have heard about you and have seen your picture...Although you were in your twenties then."

"Oh really?" He couldn't hide the elements of surprise and curiosity in his voice.

"I'll explain tomorrow. 11:30. Good-bye."

29

Uncle Jake's illness was now into the third month. Finally the doctor had some news for Rachel, but as he spoke she was only able to catch a few phrases as he explained "A Non-Hodgkin's Lymphoma." "Something called Mantle Cell lymphoma." "Very rare." "It occurs in only ten percent of the lymphoma cases." "I've called in an oncologist." "Incurable." *The prognosis was very poor and nothing could be done to save him.*

"Rachel, you'll need to talk with the oncologist to determine what the plans are, if any, for chemotherapy."

Rachel juggled calls to the doctors while she parked herself at the dining room table surrounded by Jake's mail. The VISA bill again. Only this time there were listings of charges made at locations in New York City while Jake was in the hospital. She was certain his credit card had been stolen. Annoyed and bothered by this additional distraction, she called the bank.

"…I'll check but there's another signator on the account," the customer service agent said.

"Another signator?!" The surprise in Rachel's voice was too obvious. "Can you tell me the name?"

"No, I'm not at liberty to give out that information," came the expected reply.

"But I have his Power of Attorney."

"You'll have to send us the papers before we can release any information to you."

Waving the bill in her hand, Rachel paced to and fro from the kitchen to the dining room. Her mind was reeling. It's a long shot, she thought, but there have been a lot of things she hadn't known about her uncle. Jake had so successfully compartmentalized his life that even his closest family was oblivious to all the facets and faces of his existence. She searched the black file box that contained all of Uncle Jake's personal papers and took out his little brown phone book. She found the number she was looking for under 'S.'

"Hi, this is Rachel, Jake's niece."

"Hello, Rachel."

Before Tanya could continue Rachel started talking. "I just wanted to let you know what's been going on. Jake has been moved back to the nursing home. You know Jake recently went through three biopsies. Well, unfortunately, the biopsy on the lymph node came back positive and the result is that he has lymphoma. Something called Mantle Cell lymphoma."

"What kind?" Tanya questioned.

"Mantle Cell lymphoma. Mantle, like Mickey Mantle. I don't know anything about it yet. I'll know more in a day or so. I'm trying to learn whatever I can about it. Perhaps you can do some research also and let me know."

"Of course."

With trepidation, Rachel then continued. "Listen, I need to ask you a personal question."

"Yes?" The European accent was pronounced.

"Do you, by any chance, share a credit card with my uncle?"

Softly, she replied, "Yes, I do." Quickly she added. "Let me explain, Rachel." She took a deep breath. "Your uncle is a very generous man. When I came to this country in 1986 from Poland, I came with my daughter. I could not get any credit at the time and your uncle helped me out. I had an arrangement with him and I would pay him back."

"Well, Tanya, stop using the account," Rachel instructed. "I'm closing it immediately."

"I understand. Will you let me know what's happening with Jake? He can't accept my calls anymore and I am quite worried." For someone who expressed such concern, why hadn't she visited Uncle Jake?

Rachel spent each passing day dissecting her uncle's life, one layer at a time. She relied on her intuition, detaching herself from the niece-uncle relationship that she had known since she was born.

Rachel had guessed correctly. Jake shared a credit card with a woman…this…this Tanya Stanvic who no one in the family had ever heard of before. Things were unraveling and getting more bizarre. A bizarre illness. An unknown relationship. Rachel kept learning more and more about her uncle's life that she wasn't sure she wanted to know…

"Tanya keeps calling. All your friends are really concerned about you!" Rachel leaned over Uncle Jake so he could hear her and she could look directly into his blue eyes. His eyes seemed glassier. Was there any understanding behind them?

He was not totally coherent, but strained to answer. "Where is Anna going to school?" Jake whispered.

Anna? Tanya's daughter?

"I don't know. She didn't mention it."

"She was going to New York University but didn't feel it was…it was…good enough…Wanted to transfer to Columbia." Jake nodded his head slowly. "Smart girl…"

NYU? Not good enough?

"Jake, I have to talk to you about what the doctors told me." Rachel walked to the other side of his bed, by the window and held the bedside rail as she crouched down to be face to face.

"The results of the biopsies are in. They found the lymph node to be malignant. It's a lymphoma. I'm sorry…The doctors are talking about chemotherapy."

His eyes widened, his blue eyes bulged from his head, and his eyebrows rose on his forehead. "Why haven't they spoken with me about this?"

"They have. Apparently, you tend to forget things." She looked him straight in the face.

He barely nodded. Looking very depressed and tired, he closed his eyes and turned his face the other way into the pillow. Rachel sat there holding his arm for a while.

"I love you, Uncle Jake." Although she was choked up holding back her tears, she spoke the words clearly enough for him to hear. "I love you." She didn't know what else to say.

Rachel sat in the only chair in the room for a while until she heard him snore, then slowly, quietly, left the room. She walked down the corridor with tears flowing freely down her cheeks. She knew her uncle no longer understood or was capable of mentally processing anything she said.

The kitchen picture was askew so Rachel tapped it into place. Abby was in the kitchen, drawing with colored pencils. Adam was in the den playing Gameboy.

"I'm making this for you, Mommy," Abby said with pride.

"Thank you, sweetheart." Rachel's heart was warmed by Abby's sweet gesture. "Abby, do you think you can move to the other table to finish? We have to get dinner ready."

Abby bounced off to another room.

"Why did you chase her out?" David snapped.

"Stop it, David. I didn't chase her out. Please, stop it. I also had a bad day. Guess who I had the pleasure to speak with?" Rachel's voiced reeked sarcasm. "My sis-TER." Rachel emphatically enunciated each syllable.

"She informed me that she visited Uncle Jake last Thursday, which I had known about from the nurse. Cheryl boasted that she promised Uncle Jake that we would tell him whatever the doctors say. We wouldn't keep him in the dark."

Rachel rambled, "I don't know why I tried to explain it to her. She doesn't get it. The doctors and I do tell him *everything*. His mental state is deteriorating. He doesn't remember. You can tell him something six times and he'll ask you the same questions as if you never spoke to him about it before. We've been dealing with his state of mind for a while. How dare she think she has the right to tell us how to handle things just because *her highness* breezed in for a few hours to visit!"

"And then she had the audacity to tell me she is only trying to help!" Rachel mimicked her sister, "If you need me to help with his apartment or something, I can come in again. I'm good at going through papers."

David nearly choked with laughter. "Good imitation, Rach! Do it again!"

Rachel ignored David's comment and kept rambling. "I told her that she doesn't have a clue as to what has been going on here. She has absolutely no inkling as to the condition of his apartment, his life, anything. What does Cheryl know about him, really? There have been lots of surprises. Did she know he shared a credit card with a lady friend no one ever knew or heard of?"

"How did you leave it with her?" David asked.

"Well, Cheryl became very quiet. Eventually she said, 'I guess you have everything under control then. If you want to talk or tell me something, you know how to reach me.'"

"Fat chance," Rachel mumbled just loud enough for David to hear.

David usually had very little time to spend on the phone. His dental practice was thriving and he needed more office help. He did call home just after lunch knowing Rachel did not have any scheduled classes to teach. "Uncle Jake called me at the office this afternoon. He wants to see us as soon as possible. He said it's very important and he can't talk to us over the phone." David said.

"I can't go," Rachel responded. "I was just there. I'll go tomorrow." She continued to open the mail while holding the phone with her shoulder.

The call waiting beep interrupted their conversation. Rachel picked it up only to hear Uncle Jake's voice. It was a strained whisper. "Can you come over? I need to talk to you."

"Jake! I'm so glad you were able to use the phone!"

"I had the nurse dial. Why don't you leave *me* your phone number?" he asked emphatically.

Rachel didn't respond. It was of no use. He continued, "Can you come over now?"

"Can't you tell me what it's about now?"

"No. I have to see you."

"I'll see what I can do."

"Okay. Okay."

Rachel pressed the flash button and pleaded with David. "Please, can't *you* go over there this evening? I'm exhausted and I've already been there this morning. I can't handle anymore of it today."

David was also tired, but agreed. "I'll stop there after dinner on my way to the poker game."

Rachel breathed a sigh of relief. "Thanks."

The kids were home from school later in the afternoon and Abigail was looking for something to do, so Rachel had her chop the vegetables for a salad. After dinner, the kids disappeared from the table and David left for the nursing home. Rachel was left alone in the kitchen to clean up, grateful for the few minutes of solitude.

David's voice had a peculiar tone when he called about twenty minutes later. "He's bonkers tonight, Rach. When I came in he insisted he wants to talk to you because I talk too loud!" David was whispering into the phone. I heard David speak to Uncle Jake. "Yes, it's Rachel. Sure, here's the phone."

"Uncle Jake? Is everything okay?"

"I can't speak too loud. They're right outside." Jake's voice was strange.

"*Who* is outside?"

"You know. They are near the Israelis. What do you call them?"

"Arabs?"

"No, no."

"Egyptians, Uncle Jake?"

"Yeah, that's right. They've been here all afternoon. They've been talking right outside my door. I hear the whole thing. They take people out of here who don't cooperate. They've already tried to poison me with the fish."

"They're taking good care of you there, Uncle Jake."

"No, they are not!" He became even more agitated. "You don't understand. And my roommate is another one! He can't wait until I go down so he can take all my things."

Rachel didn't know how to respond. Jake was totally paranoid and completely irrational. "I promise I'll call the doctor and figure out what's going on. I'll be over there tomorrow. Put David on the phone."

Jake didn't hear me. He kept rambling, "They are all part of it. The doctors. The nurses…"

"Jake," Rachel interrupted with a strong, adamant, voice. Speaking slowly and deliberately Rachel enunciated, "Put David on the phone *now*, Uncle Jake."

She heard David's voice again. "He's gone off the deep end completely. His dementia has gotten worse."

Rachel glanced at the computer clock - 2:00 a.m. She couldn't sleep, frightened by Jake's severe paranoia. The coffee she had prepared earlier was already cold. Her eyelids were heavy and her eyes were burning as she sat staring at the computer monitor trying to understand the information about Mantle Cell lymphoma. She was clicking on links at the National Cancer Institute site, Sloan-Kettering, and any medical institution in the search results. Most of the information available was extremely technical. The only thing she really understood was that by the time the disease is diagnosed, it's too late to save the patient.

Rachel called Elizabeth at a more reasonable morning hour and tried to explain what she gleaned from all the information. Elizabeth, too, had been busy calling medical organizations desperate for information and help. Elizabeth had continued to visit with Jake every Saturday, and struggled to keep his spirits up. The dementia worsened and Rachel became more anxious about each visit.

"How much money do you have with you?" Jake asked one evening.

"Money?" Rachel repeated.

"SHHHHHH!" Jake's bony, wrinkled index finger tremored as he held it perpendicular to his lips.

"Why do you need money?" Rachel whispered.

His roommate piped in attempting to be helpful. "You can arrange to leave money at the office downstairs for things you need…like a haircut or something from the newsstand."

Jake waved his hand as if to brush off anything his roommate said. "Don't listen to him," he mouthed the words in an exaggerated, deliberate form. "He doesn't understand what's going on here."

"Jake, I *can* start an account for you if you want," Rachel offered.

"No, no." His head moved from side to side, showing disapproval. He was becoming impatient. Rachel wasn't going along with his request, but eventually relented.

"Okay. How much do you want?"

He signaled the amount by opening and closing his hands. He flashed five…ten…fifteen…twenty. "You want twenty dollars?" Rachel mouthed.

Jake nodded.

She took a twenty-dollar bill from her purse and gave it to him. "Do you want me to put it into the drawer?"

Again, he motioned "No" with his head.

He tightly clutched the twenty in his hand and slipped his arm under the blanket and closed his eyes.

The next afternoon, the oncologist, a slim man about David's age and height, with a full head of black hair parted on the side, walked off the elevator. His charcoal gray double-breasted suit hung neatly on his physique. After the obligatory introductions, he examined Jake. As he entered the room, he found Jake asleep on his back, snoring very loudly. His hair was all gray and messed up from being in bed and a few long straggly eyebrow hairs were hanging down his lid. Someone had dressed Jake in tan trousers and a plain white undershirt. The doctor touched his patient's shoulder. Jake's glassy blue eyes opened wide and he looked toward the doctor.

"Jake, I'm a doctor. I'm going to examine you."

Jake let out a strange shriek. "I don't understand! I don't understand!"

Rachel stood by Jake's bedside thinking he'd feel more at ease if he saw her. He strained his body to look past the doctor at her, but his eyes were void of any sign of recognition.

"Jake, let's roll you on your side. I want to listen to your chest," the doctor said.

"I don't understand!" Jake shouted again.

He no longer recognized anyone. He no longer knew Rachel.

In the hall, the doctor answered all of Rachel's questions professionally and compassionately. But he was adamant. He could not recommend chemotherapy because Jake was not cognitively aware of what was happening to him. Chemo was reserved for patients who understood the treatment and whose quality of life would be improved. “Rachel,” he concluded, “I’m not sure if the lymphoma caused the dementia or aggravated a pre-existing personality tendency. It is probably the illness. Regardless, I think the best advice right now is to keep your uncle as comfortable as possible.”

There was nothing else to say. Rachel was due to leave for Australia in two days.

30

"I don't understand!" reverberated in Rachel's mind and haunted her for days. The *pre-existing personality* phrase echoed in her brain. Where was that gentle, caring man she knew as her uncle? She strained to think what she really knew about him. He was a simple man, a teacher, devoted to his career, always collecting books and materials for his students. When he retired, he volunteered in museums, attended the theater, and continued his involvement with his Book Club. Other than Elizabeth, Rachel was not familiar with any of Jake's friends but had heard a few names mentioned over the years. That was it. He was always close to family and was always generous with them.

Rachel knew even less about Jake's youth. He would talk about how he immigrated to the United States from Poland before World War II. But he was five years old when he came to this country and just how much he actually remembered is a question.

Jake's father lived in New York City for close to two years before he could bring over his wife and children. So Jake didn't get to see his father at all for that period of time.

It was 1926 when they left their home in Skierniewice, Poland and traveled by train to Gadansk. There they boarded a boat to LaHavre, France, and then a ship to the United States. The ship took water soon after they left port and they had to return to LaHavre and wait for another ship. Rachel's dad was afraid to learn how to swim because of that experience. The second ship made it to New York where Jake, along with his mother and older brother, joined his father. Those early years were years of struggle; they were very poor and they lived through the Depression with great difficulty. But through it all, Rachel's father and Jake succeeded academically and they both attained master's degrees.

Jake occasionally reminisced about life during the Depression recounting how his mother washed his one pair of summer shorts and summer shirt every night so they would dry by morning. He wore one pair of shoes until they had holes in them. Yet, the family was close and very loving. Special occasions were not elaborate; simply a weekly visit from an uncle who lived on the Lower East Side. He always came with a present for his nephews, a valuable treasure—a quarter—for both Jake and his older brother. Those quarters accumulated and Jake and his brother opened bank accounts. Rachel discovered that Jake's account still existed, although the name of the bank had changed at least ten times in sixty years.

Rachel continued to examine the many photographs and documents found in Jake's apartment, touching them, staring at them, trying to solve the mystery of her uncle; to learn something more about her family.

One particular photograph of Uncle Jake wearing a World War II army uniform jogged a vague memory of a voice whispering that Jake had once served in the army. But it was all hush-hush; no one ever talked about it. He had been drafted, but never left training camp in the States, hospitalized for an unknown illness. No immediate family member ever spoke about it and no one could identify the illness. Perhaps it was pneumonia, but no one dared to venture a guess and if they knew, they didn't say.

A distant cousin was the only one who offered some explanation. "No one ever spoke about it, Rachel. When he came home he looked so ill and very thin; his face was extremely pale and drawn. His parents were so worried." Rachel now wondered whether Jake had suffered some sort of emotional breakdown.

Sadly, that was all she knew about Jake, which didn't amount to much. She missed his laugh and the heartfelt joy he would exude as he would listen to anecdotes about Abby and Adam. She missed his unconditional, fatherly love and his willingness to do just about anything for them. Now his mind and body lacked substance, his soul barely hanging on. He had been reduced to a stranger.

31

The landing in Sydney was relatively smooth and Rachel, exhausted, was thankful to be off the plane. With limited time before boarding the next flight to Melbourne, Rachel checked the airport shops and bought something to eat. The short flight from Sydney to Melbourne was far roomier with seats in business class. Rachel met her contact by baggage claim, then drove about forty-five minutes—on the wrong side of the road, Rachel chuckled—to the hotel.

Through e-mail correspondence prior to the trip, Rachel had accepted an invitation to join a family for Shabbat dinner. The hotel wake-up call after a two-hour nap startled her; she had been in a deep sleep, alone, and in a comfortable bed for the first time in over twenty-four hours. Her mind and body had gone limp.

The cold night air was startling in July. But looking above, Rachel knew the sky was a different sky from the one David was seeing at home. They were halfway around the world from each other, yet the familiar aroma of the Sabbath meal was a source of comfort and Rachel joined in the blessings and the singing.

She was one of many guests that evening, some from Europe, some from Hong Kong, all seated in the sunken living room tastefully decorated in a contemporary style, all engaged in lively after-dinner conversation. Rachel was engrossed in an animated discussion when the host slipped an envelope to her. She graciously excused herself and found a more private spot in the hallway to read the e-mail received from David that afternoon.

Dear Rachel,

We miss you. I took the kids fishing today and we caught 15 bluefish! Our freezer is now stocked with fish we can eat for months!

Everything is okay at home. Uncle Jake is the same.

Hugs and kisses from Abigail and Adam,

I Love You.

David

It was the first she heard from family in over twenty-four hours. She was relieved, although not surprised to read they were fine; David was managing quite well with the children, and Uncle Jake was the same. Rachel hoped to relax for the week and focus on Monday's presentation.

The cold air was refreshing as a few of the guests escorted her back to the hotel through the streets of Melbourne. The city was nondescript through her jaded eyes. There was nothing outstanding about it but the people were amazingly friendly and warm. Rachel was grateful the next day was Saturday so she could shake off a terrible case of jet lag.

The Vicky Market was a great place to adventure around on Sunday morning until she was required to be at the conference center at three. The Queen Victoria market was a crowded flea market filled with souvenirs, t-shirts, crafts, clothes, electronics, and all sorts of things to haggle over. It was a cold, clear day, comfortable enough for outdoor shopping followed by a casual lunch of freshly baked French bread and a chunk of Brie from the concession stand.

The cab ride to the conference center was longer than expected; yet Rachel arrived at the Center on time, exactly at three as planned. By the time Security allowed her entrance, it was already close to three-thirty. The Conference Director greeted her with a message, "Oh, Rachel, you should know, your husband called. He thought you would be here."

"Did he leave any other message?" Rachel was puzzled.

"No. He said it wasn't urgent. He probably couldn't find the tomato sauce or something like that. You know us men without our wives around…" Rachel responded with a nervous giggle but she could not dispel her worry.

Distracted, Rachel was not able to accomplish as much as she expected in the given time at the Conference Center. Back at the hotel, the message light was blinking. Her heart began to pound. The message was simply "Call home. It's urgent."

Rachel sensed it, but she didn't want to hear it.

"David?"

"Rachel!" He stated her name emphatically, and then softly said, "Are you sitting down?"

Her voice quivered. "Tell me. What happened?"

David whispered; his voice was very low. "I'm sorry, Rachel. Uncle Jake's gone."

Rachel sat on the bed and her high-pitched, short whimpering breaths developed into sobs.

David continued, "I got a call from the doctor at one in the morning, that's about four in the afternoon your time. He needed consent from family to move him from the nursing home back to the hospital since his heart was failing. I was on the phone with Mom when the call waiting tone interrupted. It was the doctor again—who told me that it was too late."

His voice was solemn. "I've already called the Rabbi and he told me who to contact at the funeral home. I've started to make arrangements, but I'm waiting to hear from Cheryl to see if she'll fly in for the funeral. I know the difficulty you had with her at Dad's funeral, but I figured that she still is a blood relative and you are out of town and all…"

"Should I take the next possible flight out? Would I be able to make it home in time?"

"No! Even the Rabbi said not to have you come back. It was almost funny, actually. He asked where you were. I told him that you were as far from here as possible without leaving the planet. Honestly, I was advised against notifying you at all. But I did promise…"

"Absolutely. Of course. I feel badly that you are the one having to make all the arrangements! And I'm so far away I can't even help. Please keep me posted and tell me what's going on. God, David, I miss you so much."

"I miss you, too. Just do great at the conference and don't worry about anything. I'll take care of it."

Rachel had difficulty talking.

"I love you, Rach."

"I love you, too. Please let me know what's going on with the arrangements and everything. Promise me."

"I think it's best if I send a fax to the hotel since I won't know when you'll be in the room."

"Thanks for doing all this, David."

"Stop thanking me, Rach."

"Okay." Her voice cracked trying to hold back more tears. "Bye." She pulled the pillow out from under the bedspread and dug her face into it.

Rachel appreciated whatever the unexplained greater force was that cushioned her from the anguish of having to deal with funeral arrangements. She felt protected from her assumed obligation to be the emotional strength for others; she had no emotional strength for herself. Rachel knew she did what she could for him in his lifetime. Now, in his death, she had to grieve alone halfway around the world.

During the conference, Rachel experienced the sensation of stepping out of her being, watching as she went through the motions of lecturing and answering questions. She found herself waiting impatiently for the hotel shuttle that would transport her back to reality.

Depressed, she lay on the bed with the blanket covering her head. Quietly a fax was slipped under the door. When room service delivered her salad, Rachel saw a sheet of paper face down on the floor.

Dear Rachel,

I've made all the arrangements for the funeral. Your sister is flying in about 11 a.m. Abigail, Adam and I will pick her up and then we'll drive to pick up Mom on our way to the cemetery. Cozy, huh?

The funeral service will be held graveside since there will be so few of us there. Mom and I have tried to contact as many family members and his friends as possible.

Don't worry about anything. We'll talk more when you get back.

Love from the kids,

I Love You.

David

Rachel read the fax repeatedly and knew David had unknowingly designed an explosive situation. She became preoccupied with how she would have to cope with the consequences of this situation when she returned.

David spoke to Rachel frequently before the funeral. Rachel's frustration mounted and it was obvious only to her that the tensions between her mom and Cheryl would be unmanageable without her there acting as referee. But the part of Rachel that realized she had been spared that role because of geographical distance prevailed, evident by the bounce in her walk as she spent some time by the main street shops near the hotel. She stood with her back straight and head held high. It was a brisk, clear morning—her last in Melbourne—as she lifted her head toward the sky and spoke silently to the generations past; in a poignant moment she will remember for a lifetime. *I really tried for him. I didn't know what else to do. I had to rely on what the doctors told me. I really did my best...Please look after him.*

The luggage was in the hotel lobby by the time she returned along with another fax from David. This time he had written what looked like a dissertation! Four single-spaced, typed pages—which gave Rachel plenty to read during the half-hour ride to the airport. The privacy the cab ride afforded Rachel was perfect for her personal moments with David's words.

July 14, 1998

Dear Rachel,

I hope that the conference went well yesterday. I am sure that you really put on quite a show.

I know that it was hard for you to be so far away when all this was going on so I am faxing you this description of events.

As you know I first got a call from the doctor at about 1 AM Sunday morning. By 1:20, Uncle Jake was gone. Almost immediately, I got your Mom and Rabbi Herzog involved. And, following the rabbi's advice, I called the funeral home straight away.

By now it was close to 3:00 and I finally was able to reach you by phone. I am sorry that I had to break the news to you that way, Rach; but what choice did I have? But there I was, trying to do my best to arrange the burial and the funeral service, etc. I dragged myself to synagogue later that morning to speak with the rabbi in person.

"Are there any out of town relatives?" he asked me. "Because if there aren't, it would be best to have the burial **this** afternoon." At first, I answered no, but then it hit me that Cheryl would probably fly in for the funeral. I had left a voice mail for her earlier saying that I urgently needed to speak with her and I rushed home to try to speak to her directly.

When eventually we spoke, Cheryl confirmed that she would indeed fly in; but could not get on a flight until Monday morning. I tracked down Rabbi Herzog to tell him that we want to have the funeral Monday afternoon as late as possible.

Next, I called your Mom to tell her. Rach—She went ballistic!

"How dare you make plans with Cheryl before consulting me," she yelled into the phone. "How could you have even thought of making the funeral on Sunday?" and so on...

But wait Rach; the best was yet to come. Cheryl and I spoke several times over the next hour or so and we finalized her flight arrangements. I told her that I would pick her up at the airport on my way down to get your Mom. That did it!

Mom was really furious now. She told me quite adamantly that she would not get into a car with Cheryl so she will drive herself to the funeral! In the meantime, I had a meeting with the funeral director (What a pleasant guy he was! I guess he only deals with people who never argue). He asked me all kinds of questions, Rach, about what kind of casket to use (he actually showed me a catalog!) and whether we would be placing an obit in "The Tribune" and "The Times."

Well, I did the best I could, obviously. (Mom would later ask me why I didn't include her in the planning. My answer simply was that I was here and she wasn't.) The Funeral Home director promised to make all the arrangements. We planned to hold the funeral Monday at 4 p.m. I soon got a call from the director. "The last burial at the cemetery is at 2:30. Some kind of New Jersey Union thing." We had to call the funeral for 2:15.

First I called Cheryl to make sure that she can arrive in time. She said she would call me right back. Next, I had to track down Herzog to make sure that he could make it to officiate that early. He said he could not; some function that he couldn't get out of. In a panic, I tried to call Rabbi Rosen to see if he could make himself available. Finally I tracked him down and he said he was officiating at another funeral! I even had Mom call Rabbi Hoffman in New York to enlist his help. No dice. Finally, Rabbi Herzog did call back and thankfully was able to rearrange his schedule. He would be there.

I ended the evening calling names in Jake's address book. Lots of names. Lots and lots of names.

Names we never heard of before now. I told them who I was and gave the funeral arrangement information. I even called Cousin Max, but there was no way that he could get a flight from the west coast in time.

I was in bed Sunday evening and Mom called. Although she didn't want to go with Cheryl and me, she relented only because her car needed repair. (Lucky me!)

I woke early this morning and planned to drive Adam to camp. (I made arrangements with Julie to pick him up this evening. She is such a good friend.) As far as Abigail went, I gave her the choice—she could go with me to the funeral or she could go to camp. She chose the former. I was really proud of her.

Well, Adam got dressed readily enough but insisted that he wanted to go to the funeral also. Rachel, I deliberated for a while about this but I decided that he is already over 9 years old and he was so close to Uncle Jake that if he wanted to pay his respects in this way, that I should allow him to go with us to the funeral.

I had to see a few patients at the office and planned to leave at around noon to pick up the kids. We made pretty good time traveling to the airport and I was able to recognize Cheryl. She's really lost a lot of weight, Rach. You would be shocked!

In the car, Adam asked her a lot of embarrassing questions about your childhood and I really think that your sib enjoyed this immensely. So it was a pleasant ride for Cheryl and the kids.

This all changed when we got to your mom. Cheryl vacated the front seat to allow Mom to go in, but Mom walked right by her as if she didn't exist and sat in the back with the kids. This behavior and her icy cold stares shocked even Abby.

This continued throughout the ride to the cemetery. Mom ignored Cheryl and asked me all kinds of questions about the funeral arrangements. Of course this also meant tirades of criticism about the way things were planned.

In time, we arrived at the cemetery and saw that we were the second car to arrive. Your cousins Mark and Eileen were already waiting. Mom literally bolted out of the car to wait with them without saying a word.

Slowly, others began to arrive. Sue and Eddie came over to offer me their condolences. I have to tell you, Rach, that Sue's voice sounds so much like yours! She's your what—second cousin?

Anyway, his friends from his book club and the Shakespeare Society came to introduce themselves to me. They all said he was a wonderful man.

Then, I saw a rather chic-looking woman walking toward me. I'd say she was fifty-ish, wearing a huge straw hat that covered most of her brown wavy hair. You could tell she must've been really beautiful when she was younger. Her most pronounced feature was her almond shaped eyes.

As she approached, she said, "You must be David," in a heavily Eastern European accented voice. "I am Tanya. I was a good friend of your uncle."

She took my hand and looked me in the eyes. "Thank you for calling me last night. Jake was a very special man..."

The service was really beautiful and quite touching. Rabbi Herzog spoke about how Uncle Jake was such a giving and generous man and how devoted he was to his homebound students. Even though he never really got to know him, Herzog spoke of Jake as if they were well acquainted for many years.

I stood back to take in the scene of this eclectic, but small group of friends and relatives who had assembled to say farewell to our Uncle Jake. As the crowd began to break up, your mom was whisked away into Mark's car leaving me to try to comfort the kids.

We drove home and I couldn't help thinking about how Jake had finally joined your dad and grandparents after all those lonely years.

Rachel—have a good flight back. We all miss you. Our love and condolences.

We will see you very soon,

David

A strand of hair clung to the tear on Rachel's cheek. She swallowed hard and felt her throat burning. She had wanted to be with her family for the funeral but, at the same time, she did not want to be there.

After reading David's account, it was difficult to admit that there wasn't anything more she could do to make it easier for her family. She was at the airport now, heading for the gate, when she consciously decided to set all that aside and make the rest of the trip an enjoyable one.

It was easier to do than she expected. The city on the harbor was beautiful; the water sparkled with reflections of the buildings and skyscrapers of the city. *I could easily live here; start all over.* Fantasies popped into her mind without provocation. Focus on nothing and the mind runs wild with imagination, an absolute mental luxury.

Four days in Sydney came and went too fast, replete with tours and all-inclusive adventures in the Rainforest, the Bush and the wilds of the Blue Mountains. She bid the kangaroos goodbye and faced an eternal twenty hour flight back to New York alone, feeling only apprehension about what she would uncover upon her return home.

32

Reality can be agonizing. Rachel heard all the complaints she expected. Mom was angry with David for insisting on having both her and Cheryl in the car on the way to the funeral. Cheryl made sure to slip in *her* opinion "…Not to make you feel bad, Rachel, but it would have been easier had you been there…"

Rachel just couldn't be bothered. She only cared about how all this affected Abby and Adam. She knew Abby had cried uncontrollably at the cemetery and Rachel felt bad enough that she hadn't been there to hold her. Hopeful that her mom and sister could act like adults for a few hours was a gross overestimation of their characters and Rachel was left to pick up the pieces. Aside from all the emotions, Rachel was still responsible for making some sense out of Jake's life by going through his mail, papers and apartment.

The VISA bill, again. This time it was unmistakable that Tanya was still charging to Jake's account even after Rachel emphatically instructed her to stop. If there had been some repayment arrangement, Rachel wanted to know how it worked, but she'd wait a week or so until she could recuperate from jet lag. Being wide awake at three in the morning gave her plenty of time to think, to review Jake's papers without being disturbed. The downside, of course, was that Rachel was fast asleep by four in the afternoon...

Rachel's days were filled with detective work. She had turned to her trusted lawyer, Claire Weils, a long-time friend. The months of reading Jake's mail and finding account statements, bankbooks and stock certificates, gave Rachel some inkling as to the size of the estate. But no one had a clue as to the true amount, so with her lawyer, Rachel embarked on a massive search. If stocks were missing, they had to find them. If bank accounts or safety deposit boxes existed, they needed to know where. And so the search progressed as Rachel learned more about businesses and estates in a few months than most learn during three years of law school. What was remarkable to Rachel was that wherever she searched, more assets were found. And as the estate total increased, Rachel acted as though it was all a game of Monopoly. Yet each piece of paper from Jake's apartment held more clues about him.

It was now autumn in Connecticut; the leaves were turning spectacular rich shades of reds and oranges as the greens faded. As Claire examined Jake's checkbook register with Rachel, they noticed that large sums had been paid out to an Optima charge card, a card not yet found. The attorney called to cancel the card.

"…Yes, I'm the attorney representing his estate…what do you mean there's no record of his name or social security number?" Claire was a sophisticated woman in her fifties, with properly coiffed short brown hair, wearing a tailored lavender suit. She balanced the phone in her right hand, and readied her pen in her left as she looked up at Rachel, quizzically. She concentrated on the phone conversation. "Have you checked all the databases…even the accounts that may have been closed? Okay, let me give you the account number. Just a minute."

Rachel scurried to find the number for her, grabbing the envelope that contained a bank statement with cancelled checks. The account number was written along the top of one of the checks in Jake's familiar handwriting.

"We have the number. Thank you for waiting. It's 3215 0046 4432 3329…Sure, I'll hold."

After a few minutes of being on hold, Claire was engaged in conversation again. "The account is not in his name? Does he have signing privileges? No, hmmm. Okay." She was thinking fast on her feet. "How about if I give *you* a name and you tell me yes or no." She spelled it out…"Tanya Stanvic—S - T - A - N - V - I - C."

"Okay, thank you very much," she concluded the conversation as her head was furiously bobbing up and down indicating their instincts were correct.

Rachel reacted, "You mean he not only shared his Visa card by giving her signing privileges, he also paid her other bills?" She was irate.

"Yes, and by the looks of his checkbook registers, he also paid her phone bills, too."

"That was close to four hundred a month." Rachel paused and thought quietly for a moment. "It's just hard to believe. In the past few months alone, I paid over eight thousand dollars to VISA and they were all her charges! Who *is* she? She told me she had an arrangement with Jake and she always reimbursed him. How am I suppose to ask her for those payments?"

"Look, if you want to try, send her a certified letter asking her for payment for the last bill. See what happens. Maybe you can get the credit card company to go after her first before they go after the money from the estate. I doubt it'll work because it was his card and she had legitimate signing privileges." She stopped for a minute, removed her glasses and rubbed her eyes. "If it made him happy while he was alive, you can't deny him that."

"But I guess it angers me because she is twenty-five years his junior and I think—no, I *know*—she was taking advantage of his generous heart. What am I supposed to think? Even after I told her to stop using the VISA card because I was closing the account, she continued to charge things for another two weeks! Look—a thousand dollars to the university her daughter is attending, another two-fifty at Benetton's—do you believe this?!" Rachel was fuming.

"Rachel, be rational. Your uncle made these arrangements with her. You don't know her and you don't know what type of relationship they had. You read about these stories of women from Eastern Europe trying to get a hold of these "sugar daddies." Just realize, though, how dramatically her lifestyle is going to change! Even if she earns thirty-five or forty thousand a year, she was getting close to sixty thousand from your uncle, tax-free! That amounts to close to one hundred thousand a year! Now she'll be forced to live within her own budget…unless she latches on to another man who'll support her."

Rachel was smug. "Well, *that* made me feel a lot better." The sarcasm broke the tension and they just laughed.

Rachel was resolute in wanting to know more about who Tanya was and what kind of relationship Tanya had with her uncle. It was more than curiosity; it was resentment, almost hostility, toward a woman she didn't know. Rachel's heart was certain that Tanya had taken advantage of her uncle and all she could think of was how to avenge her.

Mail addressed to Jake stuffed the mailbox daily. The bank finally responded to Rachel's initial inquiry about the VISA charge she had thought was a mistake. The documents were self-explanatory. There, on the bottom, was Tanya's signature. Now, fully understanding that it wasn't a mistake at all, Rachel examined the complete set of documents enclosed; one of which was a copy of a financial statement of responsibility that was signed by Tanya as well. At last, some proof that *she* was liable for the charges. Satisfied, Rachel now had evidence to go after Tanya for payment. But the need to know why Tanya did what she did gnawed at Rachel unrelentingly.

33

She was a sweet woman, he thought. Maybe she was a few years older than he, but very put-together with her hair perfectly coiffed and sprayed and a hint of makeup in muted colors. Her shapely figure helped her to wear her age well.

It was an emotional meeting. Was it harder for her to relay the tragic news or more painful for him to hear it?

"She's dying, Jake, and she really didn't want you to know or upset you. You've both gone on with your lives although you touched her in a way no other man has since. But there's something even more she withheld from you which is why she was always so amazed and grateful for your consistent generosity over the years. She was always curious to know how you knew about the baby since she never told you."

"Baby?"

"So you really didn't know."

"Please explain!" He demanded.

"I can't explain, but Elena can. She wrote you a letter just two days before she went into a coma. I was in the hospital when she made me promise to hand-deliver it to you. She wanted me to see you in person. And she knew it wasn't a tremendous imposition since I visit family here frequently. My son married and moved here about four years ago. Listen, all I can say is that Elena gave birth to a beautiful baby girl in 1948. I watched her grow up into a sophisticated, educated young lady. I think the explanation you want is written here."

Marguerite lifted an envelope from her purse that was by her side on the vinyl bench seat. She stretched her arm across the table to hand it to Jake. His hand trembled as he hesitantly accepted it. All the strength in his body drained; he could barely grasp the envelope.

"Go ahead. Please take it. You know that Elena always loved you and she never wanted to burden you in any way," Marguerite added.

"Yes," Jake responded softly. His voice was distant. The lump in his throat was so large he couldn't swallow. His short breaths became more rapid. He reached into his pants pocket for his handkerchief and dried his moist eyes. "I think it's best that I read this later. Thank you for keeping your word to Elena."

His composure returned enough to act gentlemanly and he paid for Marguerite's lunch. They spoke for a short while during which Marguerite explained that really, her name was Miriam, but after the war and even after she married an American diplomat, she did not feel safe using her given name. She was careful not to speak about Elena sensing how unsteady Jake was and how he was trying to put on a pleasant face until it was socially appropriate for him to leave. She felt for him. It was so sad, so tragic, she thought. They obviously felt so deeply for each other, yet fate reigned; Jake and Elena were never meant to be together.

34

Three and a half months passed since Uncle Jake's death. The thought of returning to his apartment made Rachel's stomach turn. The job of totally clearing out his place had to be completed, which meant two more visits, one to prepare for the shoveling session—to determine what needed to be saved and what needed to be tossed—and one to have the waste management crew throw it out.

David and Rachel went through the apartment again before the scheduled clean-up crew but far more efficiently than before. When the closets were no longer blocked by garbage, they went through every article of clothing, every jacket.

"Hey, Rachel. Look at this," David's voice was curious.

David had pulled out a carefully folded napkin from a suit jacket pocket and unwrapped it. Carefully placed inside the folded napkin was a stack of crisp twenty-dollar bills. David began counting.

"Don't bother now. Keep looking through his stuff. We can look at it all later." Rachel insisted.

That visit actually totaled twenty-seven hundred dollars in cash, and one condom package—all from his jacket pockets. "Well, at least he had a good time!" Rachel joked. David was quick to retort, "No, Rachel. All it means is that he *bought* it. We don't know if he ever planned to *use* it."

Rachel had learned from experience to be very careful about checking each bag before discarding it. She and David worked feverishly to check through all the brown paper bags in plastic supermarket bags still carpeting the apartment. Among the discoveries were sterling silver wine cups etched with intricate designs engraved with Rachel's grandfather's initials, dated 1894—her grandfather's birth date. Rachel imagined her great grandfather using the wine cups in honor of her grandfather's bris. *How ironic that Jake's last trip to the synagogue was to remember his father and now he is with him,* Rachel thought. Also discovered in the bedroom armoire hidden among Rachel's grandmother's lingerie were packages of old European-style silverware wrapped in layers of plastic bags and held together tightly with two rubber bands—at the top and the bottom—the type of wrapping that was her grandmother's signature. More rummaging yielded the rest of the set, the silver serving pieces engraved with her grandmother's initials. Rachel paused, her heart ached knowing that she was the first to touch the items that had been last touched by her grandparents, the same few cherished items her grandparents brought to this country as immigrants. Now her grandparents and their children were all gone.

David continued to check old envelopes of all shapes and sizes. Old coins were found wrapped in old tissues and rubber banded together. Old stamps were found in envelopes along with junk mail. Everything had been randomly dropped. What type of personality disorder or illness could cause him to have lived like this? The question gripped Rachel's thoughts.

So much was yet unknown, maybe time would fill in the answers. She continued to work at a furious pace with the clean-up crew the following day, determined to completely clear out the apartment. She stopped and froze as she held two dusty, brownish envelopes in her hands. They were practically disintegrating in front of her eyes. The envelopes contained letters written in Yiddish, a language she could read but not understand. The return addresses written in English explained it all. One address was from the Jewish Agency, British Zone. The other was from the Jewish Agency, U.S. Zone. Both were from Bergen-Belsen. The letters were carefully placed in her purse, letters that would join the others safely stored in a box at home, until some future time when they would be translated.

More personal treasures were found. Rachel realized she was stepping through a hundred years of family history, all in one place, unearthed like an archaeological dig. Beaded dresses circa 1930, textbooks, scfarim—religious texts in Hebrew with copyrights from 1892, 1912, 1922. Six bookcases stuffed with old books, cartons and cartons of books including books in Yiddish, even Cervantes in its original Spanish. An old baby doll was uncovered, stored for a lifetime in her grandmother's dresser. Rachel couldn't determine how old it was, but as she touched the delicately molded finger, it cracked and peeled in her hand. It must have been a beautiful doll when new, complete with moveable eyelids.

After what seemed an eternity, the impossible was achieved. Rachel finally saw the apartment completely void of garbage. Only the thick dust and soot remained. And lastly, the finale was when the super broke the lock to Jake's storage bin in the basement and those bags and cartons were put directly into the dumpster. End of job. That was it.

Rachel prayed she did the right things. She hoped her grandparents were looking upon her favorably and smiling.

As she went about her evening routine before going to bed, David sensed Rachel's self doubt. "You did a great job, Rach. Of course, you know, your grandparents are giving your uncle a hard time for leaving it all up to you to clean."

Rachel struggled to smile.

35

It was a quiet night in the house. The children were busy doing their own things and David was at his Wednesday night poker game. Rachel was resting in the bedroom but by nine o'clock the urge was too great to resist. Jake's little brown telephone book was in the black file box. Again she turned to that familiar listing under 'S.' Rachel dialed the home number first and left a message on the machine. She then dialed the work number. Another answering machine, only this time Rachel's message wasn't polite, not terribly nasty, but effective enough. Rachel craved the opportunity to confront her, hungered for answers about who she was and why Uncle Jake helped support her.

It wasn't even twenty minutes later when the phone rang. Rachel was surprised that Tanya had responded so promptly but was annoyed that *she* had the audacity to complain about the tone in Rachel's message. "I don't know why you are being so hostile, Rachel. If this is about the money, your uncle would be rolling in his grave," Tanya began, defensively.

"Hold it, Tanya." Rachel was incredulous. "*You're* the one who no one knew about. You're the one who got all her bills paid by my uncle. Why didn't you just tell me the truth? Have you no remorse for lying to me!? You told me you had an arrangement with him and you would check your records to see how much you've already paid! Now *that* is misleading, no…it's just plain deceitful," Rachel scolded.

"Perhaps. But you're being so hostile. You have no idea about the relationship we had." Tanya fired back.

"You're right," Rachel immediately interrupted and in a patronizing voice added, "So why don't you tell me?" Rachel so enjoyed having the upper hand with her.

Tanya's voice softened. "I did want the chance to tell you. Why don't we meet for lunch? I do want to meet you and would prefer to tell you in person." Rachel could almost feel her squirm but was surprised Tanya continued her attempt to get sympathy.

"Why don't we *not*," Rachel snipped. "With my schedule and the kids, I'm way too busy to travel into New York for lunch with you. Why don't you just tell me *now*, on the phone."

She paused, then cleared her throat, "Okay," she relented. There was an even longer pause. She spoke slowly and deliberately. "Jake loved me. We first met in 1986 and he fell madly in love with me. He even asked me to marry him, but I didn't want to, having been through a divorce and a move to a new country and all. I just didn't want to marry again."

"I find your story hard to believe," Rachel held back a laugh. "You do not share his faith and he was a man who was so devoted to Jewish tradition."

"We did talk about the possibility of me converting. I just didn't want to marry again," Tanya tried to explain. *This lady must be delusional*, Rachel concluded. But she listened as Tanya continued her story.

"He was such an unusual man. So generous. So kind. He was like a husband and a brother to me all in one and like a father to Anna. He was part of the family. I knew all about his friends; I certainly heard a lot about you and your children. He adored your family, you know. He always spoke about Abigail and Adam as if they were his own grandchildren. I also knew about his close friend, Elizabeth. But, please, don't ever tell her about me. I don't want her hurt at all after all these years."

This was all unbelievable to Rachel, yet she didn't hang up…

"He was so giving, so unlike any other man. You know men—they always expect something in return. But we never had a sexual relationship. That's what was so unique. Ours was a deep friendship. Anna and I have lost someone very dear to us."

Yeah. You lost your free meal ticket, lady, Rachel thought.

"If you cared so deeply, why didn't you ever visit him?" Rachel challenged.

"I always respected his wishes and he said it wasn't necessary for me to come."

"You know *Elizabeth* was with him every week and was with him the day he died," Rachel wanted to rub salt in her wounds.

Tanya either didn't understand Rachel's bitter, sarcastic, condescending intonations or she chose to ignore it. Her response was surprisingly gracious. "I'm glad he had Elizabeth there with him and she was a source of support for him."

But Tanya did realize Rachel wasn't swayed by her justifications. She continued to try. "Look I don't know what you think, but…"

Rachel couldn't listen anymore and at that point the emotions, the anger, poured through the floodgates. "Tanya, let me tell you what I think. You know I had to laugh when you spoke with me when Jake was ill and you said you felt badly that someone so young had to deal with this responsibility. Tanya…I am *not* much younger than you! What am I *supposed* to think? You teach literature. You're fifty and he was *seventy-five*." She made sure to clearly enunciate *seventy-five.* "What would come to *your* mind?"

Tanya's voice was shaky. "I know. But it wasn't like that. I didn't even know how old he was until I asked your sister at the funeral! You have to understand. He really cared for me. For us. When he had that scare back at the end of last year, he even spoke to me at the time concerned for what would happen to us should he become ill. I thought it was something in the mouth because he kept going back to the dentist."

The dentist? Rachel had heard enough; her patience was worn. Both family and friends knew Jake had to go through a prostate biopsy. And Tanya hadn't known anything about it.

Rachel ended the conversation. Now more than ever Rachel yearned for some way to even the score with the woman who took advantage of her uncle's kind nature and his generosity. Eleven years of credit card charges and monthly phone bills. Close to six hundred thousand dollars worth of bill payments handed to this woman. Getting even became an obsession.

"Can't I call the IRS? After all, she's received thousands of dollars in income without paying any tax!" What a perfect way to aggravate *her*.

Claire was especially serious. "You don't even want to think about starting up with the IRS. They'll look to the estate first to collect gift tax on all those thousands of dollars. Forget it. Just remember, she's living a much different lifestyle now. Just leave it alone, Rachel."

With enormous patience and wisdom, Claire continued, "Look, your uncle was a wonderful man. Look at what he's left for you and the children! If he got some happiness from his friendship with this woman, it was *his* life and not for you to judge. Just relax. Let's get down to business."

Just moments before, Rachel had marched into Claire's law office barely able to see over the cartons and two briefcases of paperwork she was carrying. Copies of stock certificates, responses to inquiries, assessments of his personal property and bonds, all the mutual funds, IRAs, annuities, bank accounts and life insurance values, were entered into the spreadsheet as they worked together non-stop for hours. Papers and brown accordion files covered every square inch of the conference table. By day's end, there was some sense of organization. When the estate papers were organized and the amounts totaled, Rachel understood that her Uncle Jake, the simple, retired teacher from New Rochelle—the man who complained about supermarket prices—was a millionaire and no one, not even he, had known…

36

Tears rolled down his cheek. He let them. He was in the privacy of his own apartment, seated at the edge of the bed, hunched over, re-reading the last letter Elena had written:

My darling Jake,

I asked my dear friend, Marguerite, to locate you in New York. I assume that you have met and are reading this after learning the news I found so difficult to keep from you all these years. I always wrote to you that you are a part of me. What I didn't specify was that together, we did make a life. Your daughter was born November 9, 1948. During my pregnancy my father was deeply concerned about me, about my physical and mental health. But your letters and books continually arrived and just knowing you were thinking of us kept me going. My father loved the baby and she kept him alive in more ways than she'll ever know.

For a while, I really thought you found out about her somehow. You've always been so generous to us throughout the years. Your generosity helped support your daughter and we were able to educate her at a fine university. She studied humanities and loves literature, especially Shakespeare.

No, Jake, she does not know anything about her father. Henri accepted her when he married me. He was a good provider and just assumed that my work and bonuses helped to provide Tanya with a better education and more luxuries than he could have given alone. He was very forward in his thinking that way, but I also knew that he couldn't give completely to a child who was not his, although he never made it obvious to her. But I could sense it.

Don't feel badly, Jake. Yes, there were times I could not reconcile myself with the fact that we couldn't be together. I vacillated between being angry at you and being depressed that I couldn't do anything about it. I was so unsure of things and I dreamt of traveling to New York to find you. But I was afraid. I was afraid of your reaction and of being rejected. As I made my life with Henri and Tanya, I realized that you and your family could not, in any way, handle the dilemma of marrying outside your faith. In 1947, you felt compelled to find out what happened to your relatives during the war—family who perished just because they practiced the Jewish faith. I came to understand that you could not possibly introduce a non-Jewish woman into the family. Marguerite helped me so much to understand the unspoken expectations within the Jewish family. Over the years, I tried to instill in Tanya a respect for other faiths and traditions. Marguerite was especially helpful with Tanya and would invite her over to cook or bake. That gave Marguerite the opportunity to teach Tanya a little about Jewish tradition. And Tanya was so thrilled to come home with a platter filled with her culinary creation! In so many ways, Marguerite was friend and teacher to us both. I'm glad you finally met her.

Tanya married here in 1974. In 1979, she gave us a granddaughter. Unfortunately, Tanya's marriage did not work out. However, it might be a blessing in disguise. Recently, she was offered a visiting adjunct professorship in the Literature department at a state university in New York...

I know it is a big shock and a huge imposition or assumption that you'll want to...but my health is failing me, Jake. Please, please, keep an eye on our family. I know I will not see them again, but through them, perhaps we can continue to share our lives. But please, spare them the knowledge of what really happened.

Marguerite can lead you to them...

I'll always love you,

Elena

37

The complete silence that pervaded the house at 3:15 in the morning was a treasure. Rachel cherished the solitude, the sounds of silence. Abby and Adam were asleep in their rooms and David was sleeping soundly; only his breaths were audible as Rachel slowly, carefully closed the bedroom door behind her.

Stretched out in the den, Rachel surrounded herself with the old photographs and papers from Uncle Jake's apartment. It was difficult for her to assimilate all she had experienced with Uncle Jake. As a child, Rachel loved to play with him; simple games like bouncing a Spalding on a penny placed on the floor between them, or using the string from a bakery box for Cat's Cradle. Jake's laugh when he'd drop part of the string still resonated in Rachel's head. But living through his illness and death and handling his affairs after his death…the emotional confusion left her longing for answers.

Rachel studied the photographs. The many black and white portraits taken in the 1920's contained faces of ancestors—great aunts and uncles—she had known during her childhood. She turned her concentration toward the faces in the sepia photographs and strained her eyes to decipher any bit of resemblance to the faces she did recognize. She wanted to know these ancestors. She wanted to know about their lives. She wanted a connection. Rachel carefully placed the photos in a carton and knew she would need a lot more time to study them, to research her heritage, and to have the letters translated; letters that might unlock family mysteries. But she knew that it all had to be left for some time in the future. "In the not-too-distant-future," Rachel thought; the writings were already fading from the paper.

It was then Rachel understood that Uncle Jake had left her more than an inheritance. He had left her the gift of a legacy, an opportunity to unlock a family's heritage and create a connection between the past and the future. The man Rachel had known as her favorite uncle was truly faceted much like a crystal; although the lights might sometimes cause a painful glare, for most of his life, in his own simple, eccentric way he brought light to the many lives he touched.

Rachel put the carton away on the shelf in the den closet, tightened her robe and went back upstairs to the bedroom.

38

"...He was a generous man; generous of himself and generous with charity. Knowing his niece and her family, we can all have comfort knowing that his legacy lives on..."

It was a warm spring day; quite a relief after the bitter cold winter they had experienced. The few relatives and friends who had gathered around the gravesite to hear the Rabbi's eulogy for the unveiling were dispersing and returning to their cars. In her peripheral vision, Rachel saw someone approaching. An attractive woman about fifty stood before her. Her shoulder length brown hair streaked with blonde highlights was neatly combed and held in place with a headband. She wore a floral print skirt and a pastel pink cardigan over a crew neck sweater, accented only by the single strand of pearls around her neck.

"Rachel?" Rachel recognized the voice, the familiar accent.

Rachel turned. "Yes," she answered in a solemn voice.

"I *am* sorry," Tanya said.

Rachel's eyes were piercing through Tanya. "Your deceit didn't help, you know. But thanks for the thought." They were face to face at last. Rachel wanted to tell her exactly what she thought of her. There was so much on her mind; so much she had rehearsed, just waiting for an opportunity to say it aloud. But Rachel didn't say another word. It wasn't worth the effort. She just turned away.

David accompanied Mom and the children to the car as Rachel lingered by the gravesite alone. She whispered as she read the writing on the newly placed footstone:

Jacob Kessler, 1922-1998
Beloved Brother, Uncle, Great Uncle…
and Friend

About the Author

Ms. Cahn has had a career in educational technology, media and writing for over twenty years. She has been published in a psychology review text and has published and lectured internationally about integrating technology in schools. She received her Master's degree, specializing in human development from Harvard University, and lives in Connecticut with her husband and two children. Relative Stranger is her first work of fiction.

To purchase additional copies of this book, call
1stBooks Publishing.
Toll-free, book-order hotline:
1-888-280-7715.

Book-order website:
www.1stbooks.com